Further Foolishness
Sketches and Satires on The Follies of The Day

by Stephen Leacock

Preface

Many years ago when I was a boy at school, we had over our class an ancient and spectacled schoolmaster who was as kind at heart as he was ferocious in appearance, and whose memory has suggested to me the title of this book.

It was his practice, on any outburst of gaiety in the class-room, to chase us to our seats with a bamboo cane and to shout at us in defiance:

Now, then, any further foolishness?

I find by experience that there are quite a number of indulgent readers who are good enough to adopt the same expectant attitude towards me now.

STEPHEN LEACOCK
McGILL UNIVERSITY
MONTREAL
November 1, 1916

Contents

TIMID THOUGHTS ON TIMELY TOPICS

Further Foolishness

Follies in Fiction

I. Stories Shorter Still

Among the latest follies in fiction is the perpetual demand for stories shorter and shorter still. The only thing to do is to meet this demand at the source and check it. Any of the stories below, if left to soak overnight in a barrel of rainwater, will swell to the dimensions of a dollar-fifty novel.

(I) AN IRREDUCIBLE DETECTIVE STORY

HANGED BY A HAIR OR A MURDER MYSTERY MINIMISED

The mystery had now reached its climax. First, the man had been undoubtedly murdered. Secondly, it was absolutely certain that no conceivable person had done it.

It was therefore time to call in the great detective.

He gave one searching glance at the corpse. In a moment he whipped out a microscope.

"Ha! ha! " he said, as he picked a hair off the lapel of the dead man's coat. "The mystery is now solved. "

He held up the hair.

"Listen, " he said, "we have only to find the man who lost this hair and the criminal is in our hands. "

The inexorable chain of logic was complete.

The detective set himself to the search.

For four days and nights he moved, unobserved, through the streets of New York scanning closely every face he passed, looking for a man who had lost a hair.

On the fifth day he discovered a man, disguised as a tourist, his head enveloped in a steamer cap that reached below his ears. The man was about to go on board the *Gloritania*.

The detective followed him on board.

"Arrest him! " he said, and then drawing himself to his full height, he brandished aloft the hair.

"This is his, " said the great detective. "It proves his guilt. "

"Remove his hat, " said the ship's captain sternly.

They did so.

The man was entirely bald.

"Ha! " said the great detective without a moment of hesitation. "He has committed not one murder but about a million. "

(II) A COMPRESSED OLD ENGLISH NOVEL

SWEARWORD THE UNPRONOUNCEABLE

CHAPTER ONE AND ONLY

"Ods bodikins! " exclaimed Swearword the Saxon, wiping his mailed brow with his iron hand, "a fair morn withal! Methinks twert lithlier to rest me in yon glade than to foray me forth in yon fray! Twert it not? "

But there happened to be a real Anglo-Saxon standing by.

"Where in heaven's name, " he said in sudden passion, "did you get that line of English? "

"Churl! " said Swearword, "it is Anglo-Saxon. "

"You're a liar! " shouted the Saxon, "it is not. It is Harvard College, Sophomore Year, Option No. 6. "

Swearword, now in like fury, threw aside his hauberk, his baldrick, and his needlework on the grass.

"Lay on! " said Swearword.

"Have at you! " cried the Saxon.

They laid on and had at one another.

Swearword was killed.

Thus luckily the whole story was cut off on the first page and ended.

(III) A CONDENSED INTERMINABLE NOVEL

FROM THE CRADLE TO THE GRAVE
OR A THOUSAND PAGES FOR A DOLLAR

NOTE. -This story originally contained two hundred and fifty thousand words. But by a marvellous feat of condensation it is reduced, without the slightest loss, to a hundred and six words.

(I)

Edward Endless lived during his youth
  in Maine,
    in New Hampshire,
      in Vermont,
        in Massachusetts,
          in Rhode Island,
            in Connecticut.

(II)

Then the lure of the city lured him. His fate took him to
  New York, to Chicago, and to Philadelphia.

In Chicago he lived,
  in a boarding-house on Lasalle Avenue,
  then he boarded—
  in a living-house on Michigan Avenue.

In New York he
  had a room in an eating-house on Forty-first Street,
  and then—
  ate in a rooming-house on Forty-second Street.

In Philadelphia he
  used to sleep on Chestnut Street,
  and then—

slept on Maple Street.

During all this time women were calling to him. He knew
   and came to be friends with —
      Margaret Jones,
         Elizabeth Smith,
            Arabella Thompson,
            Jane Williams,
               Maud Taylor.

And he also got to know pretty well,
   Louise Quelquechose,
      Antoinette Alphabetic,
         Estelle Etcetera.

And during this same time Art began to call him —
   Pictures began to appeal to him.
      Statues beckoned to him.
         Music maddened him,
            and any form of Recitation or Elocution drove
               him beside himself.

   (III)

Then, one day, he married Margaret Jones.
   As soon as he had married her
      He was disillusioned.
         He now hated her.

Then he lived with Elizabeth Smith —
   He had no sooner sat down with her than —
      He hated her.

Half mad, he took his things over to Arabella Thompson's flat to live
with her.

The moment she opened the door of the apartment, he loathed her.

   He saw her as she was.

Driven sane with despair, he then —

(Our staff here cut the story off. There are hundreds and hundreds of pages alter this. They show Edward Endless grappling in the fight for clean politics. The last hundred pages deal with religion. Edward finds it after a big fight. But no one reads these pages. There are no women in them. Our staff cut them out and merely show at the end—

   Edward Purified—
    Uplifted—
     Transluted.

The whole story is perhaps the biggest thing ever done on this continent. Perhaps!)

II. Snoopopaths; or, Fifty Stories in One

This particular study in the follies of literature is not so much a story as a sort of essay. The average reader will therefore turn from it with a shudder. The condition of the average reader's mind is such that he can take in nothing but fiction. And it must be thin fiction at that—thin as gruel. Nothing else will "sit on his stomach. "

Everything must come to the present-day reader in this form. If you wish to talk to him about religion, you must dress it up as a story and label it *Beth-sheba*, or *The Curse of David*; if you want to improve the reader's morals, you must write him a little thing in dialogue called *Mrs. Potiphar Dines Out*. If you wish to expostulate with him about drink, you must do so through a narrative called *Red Rum*—short enough and easy enough for him to read it, without overstraining his mind, while he drinks cocktails.

But whatever the story is about it has got to deal—in order to be read by the average reader—with A MAN and A WOMAN, I put these words in capitals to indicate that they have got to stick out of the story with the crudity of a drawing done by a child with a burnt stick. In other words, the story has got to be snoopopathic. This is a word derived from the Greek—"snoopo"—or if there never was a Greek verb snoopo, at least there ought to have been one—and it means just what it seems to mean. Nine out of ten short stories written in America are snoopopathic.

In snoopopathic literature, in order to get its full effect, the writer generally introduces his characters simply as "the man" and "the woman. " He hates to admit that they have no names. He opens out with them something after this fashion: "The Man lifted his head. He looked about him at the gaily bedizzled crowd that besplotched the midnight cabaret with riotous patches of colour. He crushed his cigar against the brass of an Egyptian tray. 'Bah! ' he murmured, 'Is it worth it? ' Then he let his head sink again. "

You notice it? He lifted his head all the way up and let it sink all the way down, and you still don't know who he is. For The Woman the beginning is done like this: "The Woman clenched her white hands till the diamonds that glittered upon her fingers were buried in the soft flesh. 'The shame of it, ' she murmured. Then she took from the table the telegram that lay crumpled upon it and tore it into a hundred pieces. 'He dare not! ' she muttered through her closed teeth. She looked about the hotel room with its garish furniture. 'He has no right to follow me here, ' she gasped. "

All of which the reader has to take in without knowing who the woman is, or which hotel she is staying at, or who dare not follow her or why. But the modern reader loves to get this sort of shadowy incomplete effect. If he were told straight out that the woman's name was Mrs. Edward Dangerfield of Brick City, Montana, and that she had left her husband three days ago and that the telegram told her that he had discovered her address and was following her, the reader would refuse to go on.

This method of introducing the characters is bad enough. But the new snoopopathic way of describing them is still worse. The Man is always detailed as if he were a horse. He is said to be "tall, well set up, with straight legs. "

Great stress is always laid on his straight legs. No magazine story is acceptable now unless The Man's legs are absolutely straight. Why this is, I don't know. All my friends have straight legs—and yet I never hear them make it a subject of comment or boasting. I don't believe I have, at present, a single friend with crooked legs.

But this is not the only requirement. Not only must The Man's legs be straight but he must be "clean-limbed, " whatever that is; and of course he must have a "well-tubbed look about him. " How this look is acquired, and whether it can be got with an ordinary bath and water are things on which I have no opinion.

The Man is of course "clean-shaven. " This allows him to do such necessary things as "turning his clean-shaven face towards the speaker, " "laying his clean-shaven cheek in his hand, " and so on. But every one is familiar with the face of the up-to-date clean-shaven snoopopathic man. There are pictures of him by the million on magazine covers and book jackets, looking into the eyes of The Woman—he does it from a distance of about six inches—with that snoopy earnest expression of brainlessness that he always wears. How one would enjoy seeing a man—a real one with Nevada whiskers and long boots—land him one solid kick from behind.

Then comes The Woman of the snoopopathic story. She is always "beautifully groomed" (who these grooms are that do it, and where they can be hired, I don't know), and she is said to be "exquisitely gowned. "

It is peculiar about The Woman that she never seems to wear a *dress*—always a "gown. " Why this is, I cannot tell. In the good old stories that I used to read, when I could still read for the pleasure of it, the heroines —that was what they used to be called—always wore dresses. But now there is no heroine, only a woman in a gown. I wear a gown myself—at night. It is made of flannel and reaches to my feet, and when I take my candle and go out to the balcony where I sleep, the effect of it on the whole is not bad. But as to its "revealing every line of my figure"—as The Woman's gown is always said to— and as to its "suggesting even more than it reveals"—well, it simply does *not*. So when I talk of "gowns" I speak of something that I know all about.

Yet, whatever The Woman does, her "gown" is said to "cling" to her. Whether in the street or in a *cabaret* or in the drawing-room, it "clings. " If by any happy chance she throws a lace wrap about her, then it clings; and if she lifts her gown—as she is apt to—it shows, not what I should have expected, but a *jupon*, and even that clings. What a *jupon* is I don't know. With my gown, I never wear one. These people I have described, The Man and The Woman—The Snoopopaths—are, of course, not husband and wife, or brother and sister, or anything so simple and old-fashioned as that. She is some one else's wife. She is *The Wife of the Other Man.* Just what there is, for the reader, about other men's wives, I don't understand. I know tons of them that I wouldn't walk round a block for. But the reading public goes wild over them. The old-fashioned heroine was unmarried. That spoiled the whole story. You could see the end from the beginning. But with Another Man's Wife, the way is blocked. Something has got to happen that would seem almost obvious to anyone.

The writer, therefore, at once puts the two snoopos—The Man and The Woman—into a frightfully indelicate position. The more indelicate it is, the better. Sometimes she gets into his motor by accident after the theatre, or they both engage the drawing-room of a Pullman car by mistake, or else, best of all, he is brought accidentally into her room at an hotel at night. There is something about an hotel room at night, apparently, which throws the modern reader into convulsions. It is always easy to arrange a scene of this sort. For example, taking the sample beginning that I gave above, The Man, whom I left sitting at the *cabaret* table, above, rises unsteadily —it is the recognised way of rising in a *cabaret*—and, settling the reckoning with the waiter, staggers into the street. For myself I never do a reckoning with the waiter. I just pay the bill as he adds it, and take a chance on it.

As The Man staggers into the "night air, " the writer has time—just a little time, for the modern reader is impatient—to explain who he is and why he staggers. He is rich. That goes without saying. All clean-limbed men with straight legs are rich. He owns copper mines in Montana. All well-tubbed millionaires do. But he has left them, left everything, because of the Other Man's Wife. It was that or madness—or worse. He had told himself so a thousand times. (This little touch about "worse" is used in all the stories. I don't just understand what the "worse" means. But snoopopathic readers reach for it with great readiness.) So The Man had come to New York (the only place where stories are allowed to be laid) under an assumed name, to forget, to drive her from his mind. He had plunged into the mad round of—I never could find it myself, but it must be there, and as they all plunge into it, it must be as full of them as a sheet of Tanglefoot is of flies.

"As The Man walked home to his hotel, the cool night air steadied him, but his brain is still filled with the fumes of the wine he had drunk. " Notice these "fumes. " It must be great to float round with them in one's brain, where they apparently lodge. I have often tried to find them, but I never can. Again and again I have said, "Waiter, bring me a Scotch whisky and soda with fumes. " But I can never get them.

Thus goes The Man to his hotel. Now it is in a room in this same hotel that The Woman is sitting, and in which she has crumpled up the telegram. It is to this hotel that she has come when she left her husband, a week ago. The readers know, without even being told, that she left him "to work out her own salvation"—driven, by his cold brutality, beyond the breaking-point. And there is laid upon her soul, as she sits there with clenched hands, the dust and ashes of a broken marriage and a loveless life, and the knowledge, too late, of all that might have been.

And it is to this hotel that The Woman's Husband is following her.

But The Man does not know that she is in the hotel, nor that she has left her husband; it is only accident that brings them together. And it is only by accident that he has come into her room, at night, and stands there—rooted to the threshold. Now as a matter of fact, in real life, there is nothing at all in the simple fact of walking into the wrong room of an hotel by accident. You merely apologise and go out. I had this experience myself only a few days ago. I walked right into a lady's room—next door to my own. But I simply said, "Oh, I beg your pardon, I thought this was No. 343. "

"No, " she said, "this is 341. "

She did not rise and "confront" me, as they always do in the snoopopathic stories. Neither did her eyes flash, nor her gown cling to her as she rose. Nor was her gown made of "rich old stuff. " No, she merely went on reading her newspaper.

"I must apologise, " I said. "I am a little short-sighted, and very often a *one* and a *three* look so alike that I can't tell them apart. I'm afraid"

"Not at all, " said the lady. "Good evening. "

"You see, " I added, "this room and my own being so alike, and mine being 343 and this being 341, I walked in before I realised that instead of walking into 343 I was walking into 341. "

She bowed in silence, without speaking, and I felt that it was now the part of exquisite tact to retire quietly without further explanation, or at least with only a few murmured words about the possibility of to-morrow being even colder than to-day. I did so, and the affair ended with complete *savoir faire* on both sides.

But the Snoopopaths, Man and Woman, can't do this sort of thing, or, at any rate, the snoopopathic writer won't let them. The opportunity is too good to miss. As soon as The Man comes into The Woman's room—before he knows who she is, for she has her back to him—he gets into a condition dear to all snoopopathic readers.

His veins simply "surged. " His brain beat against his temples in mad pulsation. His breath "came and went in quick, short pants. " (This last might perhaps be done by one of the hotel bellboys, but otherwise it is hard to imagine.)

And The Woman—"Noiseless as his step had been, she seemed to *sense* his presence. A wave seemed to sweep over her —She turned and rose fronting him full. " This doesn't mean that he was full when she fronted him. Her gown—but we know about that already. "It was a coward's trick, " she panted.

Now if The Man had had the kind of *savoir faire* that I have, he would have said: "Oh, pardon me! I see this room is 341. My own room is 343, and to me a *one* and a *three* often look so alike that I seem to have walked into 341 while looking for 343. " And he could have explained in two words that he had no idea that she was in New York, was not following her, and not proposing to interfere with her in any way. And she would have explained also in two sentences why and how she came to be there. But this wouldn't do. Instead of it, The Man and The Woman go through the grand snoopopathic scene which is so intense that it needs what is really a new kind of language to convey it.

"Helene, " he croaked, reaching out his arms—his voice tensed with the infinity of his desire.

"Back, " she iced. And then, "Why have you come here? " she hoarsed. "What business have you here? "

"None, " he glooped, "none. I have no business. " They stood sensing one another.

"I thought you were in Philadelphia, " she said—her gown clinging to every fibre of her as she spoke.

"I was, " he wheezed.

"And you left it? " she sharped, her voice tense.

"I left it, " he said, his voice glumping as he spoke. "Need I tell you why? " He had come nearer to her. She could hear his pants as he moved.

"No, no, " she gurgled. "You left it. It is enough. I can understand"— she looked bravely up at him—"I can understand any man leaving it."

Then as he moved still nearer her, there was the sound of a sudden swift step in the corridor. The door opened and there stood before them The Other Man, the Husband of The Woman—Edward Dangerfield.

This, of course, is the grand snoopopathic climax, when the author gets all three of them—The Man, The Woman, and The Woman's Husband—in an hotel room at night. But notice what happens.

He stood in the opening of the doorway looking at them, a slight smile upon his lips.

"Well? " he said. Then he entered the room and stood for a moment quietly looking into The Man's face.

"So, " he said, "it was you. " He walked into the room and laid the light coat that he had been carrying over his arm upon the table. He drew a cigar-case from his waistcoat pocket.

"Try one of these Havanas, " he said.

Observe the *calm* of it. This is what the snoopopath loves—no rage, no blustering—calmness, cynicism. He walked over towards the mantelpiece and laid his hat upon it. He set his boot upon the fender.

"It was cold this evening, " he said. He walked over to the window and gazed a moment into the dark.

"This is a nice hotel, " he said. (This scene is what the author and the reader love; they hate to let it go. They'd willingly keep the man walking up and down for hours saying "Well! ")

The Man raised his head! "Yes, it's a good hotel, " he said. Then he let his head fall again.

This kind of thing goes on until, if possible, the reader is persuaded into thinking that there is nothing going to happen. Then:

"He turned to The Woman. 'Go in there, ' he said, pointing to the bedroom door. Mechanically she obeyed. " This, by the way, is the first intimation that the reader has that the room in which they were sitting was not a bedroom. The two men were alone. Dangerfield walked over to the chair where he had thrown his coat.

"I bought this coat in St. Louis last fall, " he said. His voice was quiet, even passionless. Then from the pocket of the coat he took a revolver and laid it on the table. Marsden watched him without a word.

"Do you see this pistol? " said Dangerfield.

Marsden raised his head a moment and let it sink.

Of course the ignorant reader keeps wondering why he doesn't explain. But how can he? What is there to say? He has been found out of his own room at night. The penalty for this in all the snoopopathic stories is death. It is understood that in all the New York hotels the night porters shoot a certain number of men in the corridors every night.

"When we married, " said Dangerfield, glancing at the closed door as he spoke, "I bought this and the mate to it—for her—just the same, with the monogram on the butt—see! And I said to her, 'If things ever go wrong between you and me, there is always this way out. '"

He lifted the pistol from the table, examining its mechanism. He rose and walked across the room till he stood with his back against the door, the pistol in his hand, its barrel pointing straight at Marsden's heart. Marsden never moved. Then as the two men faced one another thus, looking into one another's eyes, their ears caught a sound from behind the closed door of the inner room—a sharp, hard, metallic sound as if some one in the room within had raised the hammer of a pistol—a jewelled pistol like the one in Dangerfield's hand.

And then—

A loud report, and with a cry, the cry of a woman, one shrill despairing cry—

Or no, hang it—I can't consent to end up a story in that fashion, with the dead woman prone across the bed, the smoking pistol, with a jewel on the hilt, still clasped in her hand—the red blood welling over the white laces of her gown—while the two men gaze down upon her cold face with horror in their eyes. Not a bit. Let's end it like this:

"A shrill despairing cry—'Ed! Charlie! Come in here quick! Hurry! The steam coil has blown out a plug! You two boys quit talking and come in here, for heaven's sake, and fix it. '" And, indeed, if the reader will look back he will see there is nothing in the dialogue to preclude it. He was misled, that's all. I merely said that Mrs. Dangerfield had left her husband a few days before. So she had—to do some shopping in New York. She thought it mean of him to follow her. And I never said that Mrs. Dangerfield had any connection whatever with The Woman with whom Marsden was in love. Not at all. He knew her, of course, because he came from Brick City. But she had thought he was in Philadelphia, and naturally she was surprised to see him back in New York. That's why she exclaimed "Back! " And as a matter of plain fact, you can't pick up a revolver without its pointing somewhere. No one said he meant to fire it.

In fact, if the reader will glance back at the dialogue—I know he has no time to, but if he does—he will see that, being something of a snoopopath himself, he has invented the whole story.

III. Foreign Fiction in Imported Instalments.

Serge the Superman: A Russian Novel

(Translated, with a hand pump, out of the original Russian)

SPECIAL EDITORIAL NOTE, OR, FIT OF CONVULSIONS INTO WHICH AN EDITOR FALLS IN INTRODUCING THIS SORT OF STORY TO HIS READERS. We need offer no apology to our readers in presenting to them a Russian novel. There is no doubt that the future in literature lies with Russia. The names of Tolstoi, of Turgan-something, and Dostoi-what-is-it are household words in America. We may say with certainty that Serge the Superman is the most distinctly Russian thing produced in years. The Russian view of life is melancholy and fatalistic. It is dark with the gloom of the great forests of the Volga, and saddened with the infinite silence of the Siberian plain. Hence the Russian speech, like the Russian thought, is direct, terse and almost crude in its elemental power. All this appears in Serge the Superman. It is the directest, tersest, crudest thing we have ever seen. We showed the manuscript to a friend of ours, a critic, a man who has a greater Command of the language of criticism than perhaps any two men in New York to-day. He said at once, "This is big. It is a big thing, done by a big man, a man with big ideas, writing at his very biggest. The whole thing has a bigness about it that is—" and here he paused and thought a moment and added—"big. " After this he sat back in his chair and said, "big, big, big, " till we left him. We next showed the story to an English critic and he said without hesitation, or with very little, "This is really not half bad. " Last of all we read the story ourselves and we rose after its perusal—itself not an easy thing to do—and said, "Wonderful but terrible. " All through our (free) lunch that day we shuddered.

CHAPTER I

As a child. Serge lived with his father—Ivan Ivanovitch —and his mother—Katrina Katerinavitch. In the house, too were Nitska, the serving maid. Itch, the serving man, and Yump, the cook, his wife.

The house stood on the borders of a Russian town. It was in the heart of Russia. All about it was the great plain with the river running between low banks and over it the dull sky.

Further Foolishness

Across the plain ran the post road, naked and bare. In the distance one could see a moujik driving a three-horse tarantula, or perhaps Swill, the swine-herd, herding the swine. Far away the road dipped over the horizon and was lost.

"Where does it go to? " asked Serge. But no one could tell him.

In the winter there came the great snows and the river was frozen and Serge could walk on it.

On such days Yob, the postman, would come to the door, stamping his feet with the cold as he gave the letters to Itch.

"It is a cold day, " Yob would say.

"It is God's will, " said Itch. Then he would fetch a glass of Kwas steaming hot from the great stove, built of wood, that stood in the kitchen.

"Drink, little brother, " he would say to Yob, and Yob would answer, "Little Uncle, I drink your health, " and he would go down the road again, stamping his feet with the cold.

Then later the spring would come and all the plain was bright with flowers and Serge could pick them. Then the rain came and Serge could catch it in a cup. Then the summer came and the great heat and the storms, and Serge could watch the lightning.

"What is lightning for? " he would ask of Yump, the cook, as she stood kneading the *mush,* or dough, to make *slab,* or pancake, for the morrow. Yump shook her *knob,* or head, with a look of perplexity on her big *mugg,* or face.

"It is God's will, " she said.

Thus Serge grew up a thoughtful child.

At times he would say to his mother, "Matrinska (little mother), why is the sky blue? " And she couldn't tell him.
Or at times he would say to his father, "Boob (Russian for father), what is three times six? " But his father didn't know.

Each year Serge grew.

Life began to perplex the boy. He couldn't understand it. No one could tell him anything.

Sometimes he would talk with Itch, the serving man.

"Itch, " he asked, "what is morality? " But Itch didn't know. In his simple life he had never heard of it.

At times people came to the house—Snip, the schoolmaster, who could read and write, and Cinch, the harness maker, who made harness.

Once there came Popoff, the inspector of police, in his blue coat with fur on it. He stood in front of the fire writing down the names of all the people in the house. And when he came to Itch, Serge noticed how Itch trembled and cowered before Popoff, cringing as he brought a three-legged stool and saying, "Sit near the fire, little father; it is cold. " Popoff laughed and said, "Cold as Siberia, is it not, little brother? " Then he said, "Bare me your arm to the elbow, and let me see if our mark is on it still. " And Itch raised his sleeve to the elbow and Serge saw that there was a mark upon it burnt deep and black.

"I thought so, " said Popoff, and he laughed. But Yump, the cook, beat the fire with a stick so that the sparks flew into Popoff's face. "You are too near the fire, little inspector, " she said. "It burns. "

All that evening Itch sat in the corner of the kitchen, and Serge saw that there were tears on his face.

"Why does he cry? " asked Serge.

"He has been in Siberia, " said Yump as she poured water into the great iron pot to make soup for the week after the next.

Serge grew more thoughtful each year.

All sorts of things, occurrences of daily life, set him thinking. One day he saw some peasants drowning a tax collector in the river. It made a deep impression on him. He couldn't understand it. There seemed something wrong about it.

"Why did they drown him? " he asked of Yump, the cook.

"He was collecting taxes, " said Yump, and she threw a handful of cups into the cupboard.

Then one day there was great excitement in the town, and men in uniform went to and fro and all the people stood at the doors talking.

"What has happened? " asked Serge.

"It is Popoff, inspector of police, " answered Itch. "They have found him beside the river. "

"Is he dead? " questioned Serge.

Itch pointed reverently to the ground—"He is there! " he said.

All that day Serge asked questions. But no one would tell him anything. "Popoff is dead, " they said. "They have found him beside the river with his ribs driven in on his heart. "

"Why did they kill him? " asked Serge.

But no one would say.

So after this Serge was more perplexed than ever.

Every one noticed how thoughtful Serge was.

"He is a wise boy, " they said. "Some day he will be a learned man. He will read and write. "

"Defend us! " exclaimed Itch. "It is a dangerous thing. "

One day Liddoff, the priest, came to the house with a great roll of paper in his hand.

"What is it? " asked Serge.

"It is the alphabet, " said Liddoff.

"Give it to me, " said Serge with eagerness.

"Not all of it, " said Liddoff gently. "Here is part of it, " and he tore off a piece and gave it to the boy.

"Defend us! " said Yump, the cook. "It is not a wise thing, " and she shook her head as she put a new lump of clay in the wooden stove to make it burn more brightly.

Then everybody knew that Serge was learning the alphabet, and that when he had learned it he was to go to Moscow, to the Teknik, and learn what else there was.

So the days passed and the months. Presently Ivan Ivanovitch said, "Now he is ready, " and he took down a bag of rubles that was concealed on a shelf beside the wooden stove in the kitchen and counted them out after the Russian fashion, "Ten, ten, and yet ten, and still ten, and ten, " till he could count no further.

"Protect us! " said Yump. "Now he is rich! " and she poured oil and fat mixed with sand into the bread and beat it with a stick.

"He must get ready, " they said. "He must buy clothes. Soon he will go to Moscow to the Teknik and become a wise man. "

Now it so happened that there came one day to the door a drosky, or one-horse carriage, and in it was a man and beside him a girl. The man stopped to ask the way from Itch, who pointed down the post road over the plain. But his hand trembled and his knees shook as he showed the way. For the eyes of the man who asked the way were dark with hate and cruel with power. And he wore a uniform and there was brass upon his cap. But Serge looked only at the girl. And there was no hate in her eyes, but only a great burning, and a look that went far beyond the plain, Serge knew not where. And as Serge looked, the girl turned her face and their eyes met, and he knew that he would never forget her. And he saw in her face that she would never forget him. For that is love.

"Who is that? " he asked, as he went back again with Itch into the house.

"It is Kwartz, chief of police, " said Itch, and his knees still trembled as he spoke.

"Where is he taking her? " said Serge.

"To Moscow, to the prison, " answered Itch. "There they will hang her and she will die. "

"Who is she? " asked Serge. "What has she done? " and as he spoke he could still see the girl's face, and the look upon it, and a great fire went sweeping through his veins.

"She is Olga Ileyitch, " answered Itch, "She made the bomb that killed Popoff, the inspector, and now they will hang her and she will die. "

"Defend us! " murmured Yump, as she heaped more clay upon the stove.

CHAPTER II

Serge went to Moscow. He entered the Teknik. He became a student. He learned geography from Stoj, the professor, astrography from Fudj, the assistant, together with giliodesy, orgastrophy and other native Russian studies.

All day he worked. His industry was unflagging. His instructors were enthusiastic. "If he goes on like this, " they said, "he will some day know something. "

"It is marvellous, " said one. "If he continues thus, he will be a professor. "

"He is too young, " said Stoj, shaking his head. "He has too much hair. "

"He sees too well, " said Fudj. "Let him wait till his eyes are weaker."
But all day as Serge worked he thought. And his thoughts were of Olga Ileyitch, the girl that he had seen with Kwartz, inspector of police. He wondered why she had killed Popoff, the inspector. He wondered if she was dead. There seemed no justice in it.

One day he questioned his professor.

"Is the law just? " he said. "Is it right to kill? "

But Stoj shook his head, and would not answer.

"Let us go on with our orgastrophy, " he said. And he trembled so that the chalk shook in his hand.

So Serge questioned no further, but he thought more deeply still. All the way from the Teknik to the house where he lodged he was thinking. As he climbed the stair to his attic room he was still thinking.

The house in which Serge lived was the house of Madame Vasselitch. It was a tall dark house in a sombre street. There were no trees upon the street and no children played there. And opposite to the house of Madame Vasselitch was a building of stone, with windows barred, that was always silent. In it were no lights, and no one went in or out.

"What is it? " Serge asked.

"It is the house of the dead, " answered Madame Vasselitch, and she shook her head and would say no more.

The husband of Madame Vasselitch was dead. No one spoke of him. In the house were only students, Most of them were wild fellows, as students are. At night they would sit about the table in the great room drinking Kwas made from sawdust fermented in syrup, or golgol, the Russian absinth, made by dipping a gooseberry in a bucket of soda water. Then they would play cards, laying matches on the table and betting, "Ten, ten, and yet ten, " till all the matches were gone. Then they would say, "There are no more matches; let us dance, " and they would dance upon the floor, till Madame Vasselitch would come to the room, a candle in her hand, and say, "Little brothers, it is ten o'clock. Go to bed. " Then they went to bed. They were wild fellows, as all students are.
But there were two students in the house of Madame Vasselitch who were not wild. They were brothers. They lived in a long room in the basement. It was so low that it was below the street.

The brothers were pale, with long hair. They had deep-set eyes. They had but little money. Madame Vasselitch gave them food. "Eat, little sons, " she would say. "You must not die. "

The brothers worked all day. They were real students. One brother was Halfoff. He was taller than the other and stronger. The other brother was Kwitoff. He was not so tall as Halfoff and not so strong.

Further Foolishness

One day Serge went to the room of the brothers. The brothers were at work. Halfoff sat at a table. There was a book in front of him.

"What is it? " asked Serge.

"It is solid geometry, " said Halfoff, and there was a gleam in his eyes.

"Why do you study it? " said Serge.

"To free Russia, " said Halfoff.

"And what book have you? " said Serge to Kwitoff.

"Hamblin Smith's *Elementary Trigonometry*, " said Kwitoff, and he quivered like a leaf.

"What does it teach? " asked Serge.

"Freedom! " said Kwitoff.

The two brothers looked at one another.

"Shall we tell him everything? " said Halfoff.

"Not yet, " said Kwitoff. "Let him learn first. Later he shall know. "

After that Serge often came to the room of the two brothers.

The two brothers gave him books. "Read them, " they said.

"What are they? " asked Serge.

"They are in English, " said Kwitoff. "They are forbidden books. They are not allowed in Russia. But in them is truth and freedom. "

"Give me one, " said Serge.

"Take this, " said Kwitoff. "Carry it under your cloak. Let no one see it. "

"What is it? " asked Serge, trembling in spite of himself.

"It is Caldwell's *Pragmatism*, " said the brothers.

"Is it forbidden? " asked Serge.

The brothers looked at him.

"It is death to read it, " they said.

After that Serge came each day and got books from Halfoff and Kwitoff. At night he read them. They fired his brain. All of them were forbidden books. No one in Russia might read them. Serge read Hamblin Smith's *Algebra*. He read it all through from cover to cover feverishly. He read Murray's *Calculus*. It set his brain on fire. "Can this be true? " he asked.

The books opened a new world to Serge.

The brothers often watched him as he read.

"Shall we tell him everything? " said Halfoff.

"Not yet. " said Kwitoff. "He is not ready. "

One night Serge went to the room of the two brothers. They were not working at their books. Littered about the room were blacksmith's tools and wires, and pieces of metal lying on the floor. There was a crucible and underneath it a blue fire that burned fiercely. Beside it the brothers worked. Serge could see their faces in the light of the flame.

"Shall we tell him now? " said Kwitoff. The other brother nodded. "Tell him now, " he said.

"Little brother, " said Kwitoff, and he rose from beside the flame and stood erect, for he was tall, "will you give your life? "

"What for? " asked Serge.

The brothers shook their heads.

"We cannot tell you that, " they said. "That would be too much. Will you join us? "

"In what? " asked Serge.

"We must not say, " said the brothers. "We can only ask are you willing to help our enterprise with all your power and with your life if need be? "

"What is your enterprise? " asked Serge.

"We must not divulge it, " they said. "Only this: will you give your life to save another life, to save Russia? "

Serge paused. He thought of Olga Ileyitch. Only to save her life would he have given his.

"I cannot, " he answered.

"Good night, little brother, " said Kwitoff gently, and he turned back to his work.

Thus the months passed.

Serge studied without ceasing. "If there is truth, " he thought, "I shall find it. " All the time he Thought of Olga Ileyitch. His face grew pale. "Justice, Justice, " he thought, "what is justice and truth? "

CHAPTER III

Now when Serge had been six months in the house of Madame Vasselitch, Ivan Ivanovitch, his father, sent Itch, the serving man, and Yump, the cook, his wife, to Moscow to see how Serge fared. And Ivan first counted out rubles into a bag, "ten, and ten and still ten, " till Itch said, "It is enough. I will carry that. "

Then they made ready to go. Itch took a duck from the pond and put a fish in his pocket, together with a fragrant cheese and a bundle of sweet garlic. And Yump took oil and dough and mixed it with tar and beat it with an iron bar so as to shape it into a pudding.

So they went forth on foot, walking till they came to Moscow.

"It is a large place, " said Itch, and he looked about him at the lights and the people.

"Defend us, " said Yump. "It is no place for a woman. "

"Fear nothing, " said Itch, looking at her.

So they went on, looking for the house of Madame Vasselitch.

"How bright the lights are! " said Itch, and he stood still and looked about him. Then he pointed at a burleski, or theatre. "Let us go in there and rest, " he said.

"No, " said Yump, "let us hurry on. "

"You are tired, " said Itch. "Give me the pudding and hurry forward, so that you may sleep. I will come later, bringing the pudding and the fish. "

"I am not tired, " said Yump.

So they came at last to the house of Madame Vasselitch. And when they saw Serge they said, "How tall he is and how well grown! " But they thought, "He is pale. Ivan Ivanoviteh must know. "

And Itch said, "Here are the rubles sent by Ivan Ivanovitch. Count them, little son, and see that they are right. "

"How many should there be? " said Serge.

"I know not, " said Itch. "You must count them and see. "

Then Yump said, "Here is a pudding, little son, and a fish, and a duck and a cheese and garlic. "

So that night Itch and Yump stayed in the house of Madame Vasselitch.

"You are tired, " said Itch. "You must sleep. "

"I am not tired, " said Yump. "It is only that my head aches and my face burns from the wind and the sun. "

"I will go forth, " said Itch, "and find a fisski, or drug-store, and get something for your face. "

"Stay where you are, " said Yump. And Itch stayed.

Meantime Serge had gone upstairs with the fish and the duck and the cheese and the pudding. As he went up he thought. "It is selfish to eat alone. I will give part of the fish to the others. " And when he got a little further up the steps he thought, "I will give them all of the fish. " And when he got higher still he thought, "They shall have everything. "

Then he opened the door and came into the big room where the students were playing with matches at the big table and drinking golgol out of cups. "Here is food, brothers, " he said. "Take it. I need none. "

The students took the food and they cried, "Rah, Rah, " and beat the fish against the table. But the pudding they would not take. "We have no axe, " they said. "Keep it. "

Then they poured out golgol for Serge and said, "Drink it. "

But Serge would not.

"I must work, " he said, and all the students laughed. "He wants to work! " they cried. "Rah, Rah. "

But Serge went up to his room and lighted his taper, made of string dipped in fat, and set himself to study. "I must work, " he repeated.

So Serge sat at his books. It got later and the house grew still. The noise of the students below ceased and then everything was quiet.

Serge sat working through the night. Then presently it grew morning and the dark changed to twilight and Serge could see from his window the great building with the barred windows across the street standing out in the grey mist of the morning.

Serge had often studied thus through the night and when it was morning he would say, "It is morning, " and would go down and help Madame Vasselitch unbar the iron shutters and unchain the door, and remove the bolts from the window casement.

But on this morning as Serge looked from his window his eyes saw a figure behind the barred window opposite to him. It was the figure of a girl, and she was kneeling on the floor and she was in prayer, for Serge could see that her hands were before her face. And as he looked all his blood ran warm to his head, and his limbs trembled even though he could not see the girl's face. Then the girl rose from her knees and turned her face towards the bars, and Serge knew that it was Olga Ileyitch and that she had seen and known him.

Then he came down the stairs and Madame Vasselitch was there undoing the shutters and removing the nails from the window casing.

"What have you seen, little son? " she asked, and her voice was gentle, for the face of Serge was pale and his eyes were wide.

But Serge did not answer the question.

"What is that house? " he said. "The great building with the bars that you call the house of the dead? "

"Shall I tell you, little son, " said Madame Vasselitch, and she looked at him, still thinking. "Yes, " she said, "he shall know.

"It is the prison of the condemned, and from there they go forth only to die. Listen, little son, " she went on, and she gripped Serge by the wrist till he could feel the bones of her fingers against his flesh. "There lay my husband, Vangorod Vasselitch, waiting for his death. Months long he was there behind the bars and no one might see him or know when he was to die. I took this tall house that I might at least be near him till the end. But to those who lie there waiting for their death it is allowed once and once only that they may look out upon the world. And this is allowed to them the day before they die. So I took this house and waited, and each day I looked forth at dawn across the street and he was not there. Then at last he came. I saw him at the window and his face was pale and set and I could see the marks of the iron on his wrists as he held them to the bars. But I could see that his spirit was unbroken. There was no power in them to break that. Then he saw me at the window, and thus across the narrow street we said good-bye. It was only a moment. 'Sonia Vasselitch, ' he said, 'do not forget, ' and he was gone. I have not forgotten. I have lived on here in this dark house, and I have not forgotten. My sons—yes, little brother, my sons, I say—have not forgotten. Now tell me, Sergius Ivanovitch, what you have seen. "

"I have seen the woman that I love, " said Serge, "kneeling behind the bars in prayer. I have seen Olga Ileyitch. "

"Her name, " said Madame Vasselitch, and there were no tears in her eyes and her voice was calm, "her name is Olga Vasselitch. She is my daughter, and to-morrow she is to die. "

CHAPTER IV

Madame Vasselitch took Serge by the hand.

"Come, " she said, "you shall speak to my sons, " and she led him down the stairs towards the room of Halfoff and Kwitoff.

"They are my sons, " she said. "Olga is their sister. They are working to save her. "

Then she opened the door. Halfoff and Kwitoff were working as Serge had seen them before, beside the crucible with the blue flame on their faces.

They had not slept.

Madame Vasselitch spoke.

"He has seen Olga, " she said. "It is to-day. "

"We are too late, " said Halfoff, and he groaned.

"Courage, brother, " said Kwitoff. "She will not die till sunrise. It is twilight now. We have still an hour. Let us to work. "

Serge looked at the brothers.

"Tell me, " he said. "I do not understand. "

Halfoff turned a moment from his work and looked at Serge.

"Brother, " he said, "will you give your life? "

"Is it for Olga? " asked Serge.

"It is for her. "

"I give it gladly, " said Serge.

"Listen then, " said Halfoff. "Our sister is condemned for the killing of Popoff, inspector of police. She is in the prison of the condemned, the house of the dead, across the street. Her cell is there beside us. There is only a wall between. Look—"

Halfoff as he spoke threw aside a curtain that hung across the end of the room. Serge looked into blackness. It was a tunnel.

"It leads to the wall of her cell, " said Halfoff. "We are close against the wall but we cannot shatter it. We are working to make a bomb. No bomb that we can make is hard enough. We can only try once. If it fails the noise would ruin us. There is no second chance. We try our bombs in the crucible. They crumble. They have no strength. We are ignorant. We are only learning. We studied it in the books, the forbidden books. It took a month to learn to set the wires to fire the bomb. The tunnel was there. We did not have to dig it. It was for my father, Vangorod Vasselitch. He would not let them use it. He tapped a message through the wall, 'Keep it for a greater need. ' Now it is his daughter that is there. "

Halfoff paused. He was panting and his chest heaved. There was perspiration on his face and his black hair was wet.

"Courage, little brother, " said Kwitoff. "She shall not die. "
"Listen, " went on Halfoff. "The bomb is made. It is there beside the crucible. It has power in it to shatter the prison. But the wires are wrong. They do not work. There is no current in them. Something is wrong. We cannot explode the bomb. "

"Courage, courage, " said Kwitoff, and his hands were busy among the wires before him. "I am working still. "

Serge looked at the brothers.

"Is that the bomb? " he said, pointing at a great ball of metal that lay beside the crucible.

"It is, " said Halfoff.

"And the little fuse that is in the side of it fires it? And the current from the wires lights the fuse? "

"Yes, " said Halfoff.

The two brothers looked at Serge, for there was a meaning in his voice and a strange look upon his face.

"If the bomb is placed against the wall and if the fuse is lighted it would explode. "

"Yes, " said Halfoff despairingly, "but how? The fuse is instantaneous. Without the wires we cannot light it. It would be death. "

Serge took the bomb in his hand. His face was pale.

"Let it be so! " he said. "I will give my life for hers. "

He lifted the bomb in his hand. "I will go through the tunnel and hold the bomb against the wall and fire it, " he said. "Halfoff, light me the candle in the flame. Be ready when the wall falls. "

"No, no, " said Halfoff, grasping Serge by the arm. "You must not die! "

"My brother, " said Kwitoff quietly, "let it be as he says. It is for Russia! "
But as Halfoff turned to light the candle in the flame there came a great knocking at the door above and the sound of many voices in the street.

All paused.

Madame Vasselitch laid her hand upon her lips.

Then there came the sound as of grounded muskets on the pavement of the street and a sharp word of command.

"Soldiers! " said Madame Vasselitch.

Kwitoff turned to his brother.

"This is the end, " he said. "Explode the bomb here and let us die together. "

Suddenly Madame Vasselitch gave a cry.

"It is Olga's voice! " she said.

She ran to the door and opened it, and a glad voice was heard crying.

"It is I, Olga, and I am free! "

"Free, " exclaimed the brothers.

All hastened up the stairs.

Olga was standing before them in the hall and beside her were the officers of the police, and in the street were the soldiers. The students from above had crowded down the stairs and with them were Itch, the serving man, and Yump, the cook.

"I am free, " cried Olga, "liberated by the bounty of the Czar— Russia has declared war to fight for the freedom of the world and all the political prisoners are free. "

"Rah, rah! " cried the students. "War, war, war! "

"She is set free, " said the officer who stood beside Olga. "The charge of killing Popoff is withdrawn. No one will be punished for it now. "

"I never killed him, " said Olga. "I swear it, " and she raised her hand.

"You never killed him! " exclaimed Serge with joy in his heart. "You did not kill Popoff? But who did? "

"Defend us, " said Yump, the cook. "Since there is to be no punishment for it, I killed him myself. "

"You! " they cried.

"It is so, " said Yump. "I killed him beside the river. It was to defend my honour. "

"It was to defend her honour, " cried the brothers. "She has done well. "

They clasped her hand.

"You destroyed him with a bomb? " they said.

"No, " said Yump, "I sat down on him. "

"Rah, rah, rah, " said the students.

There was silence for a moment. Then Kwitoff spoke.

"Friends, " he said, "the new day is coming. The dawn is breaking. The moon is rising. The stars are setting. It is the birth of freedom. See! we need it not! " —and as he spoke he grasped in his hands the bomb with its still unlighted fuse—"Russia is free. We are all brothers now. Let us cast it at our enemies. Forward! To the frontier! Live the Czar. "

Movies and Motors, Men and Women

IV. Madeline of the Movies: A Photoplay done back into Words

EXPLANATORY NOTE.

In writing this I ought to explain that I am a tottering old man of forty-six. I was born too soon to understand moving pictures. They go too fast. I can't keep up. In my young days we used a magic lantern. It showed Robinson Crusoe in six scenes. It took all evening to show them. When it was done the hall was filled full with black smoke and the audience quite unstrung with excitement. What I set down here represents my thoughts as I sit in front of a moving picture photoplay and interpret it as best I can.

Flick, flick, flick! I guess it must be going to begin now, but it's queer the people don't stop talking: how can they expect to hear the pictures if they go on talking? Now it's off. PASSED BY THE BOARD OF—. Ah, this looks interesting—passed by the board of— wait till I adjust my spectacles and read what it—

It's gone. Never mind, here's something else, let me see—CAST OF CHARACTERS—Oh, yes—let's see who they are—MADELINE MEADOWLARK, a young something—EDWARD DANGERFIELD, a—a what? Ah, yes, a roo—at least, it's spelt r-o-u-e, that must be roo all right—but wait till I see what that is that's written across the top—MADELINE MEADOWLARK; OR, ALONE IN A GREAT CITY. I see, that's the title of it. I wonder which of the characters is alone. I guess not Madeline: she'd hardly be alone in a place like that. I imagine it's more likely Edward Dangerous the Roo. A roo would probably be alone a great deal, I should think. Let's see what the other characters are—JOHN HOLDFAST, a something. FARMER MEADOWLARK, MRS. MEADOWLARK, his Something—

Pshaw, I missed the others, but never mind; flick, flick, it's beginning—What's this? A bedroom, eh? Looks like a girl's bedroom—pretty poor sort of place. I wish the picture would keep still a minute—in Robinson Crusoe it all stayed still and one could sit and look at it, the blue sea and the green palm trees and the black footprints in the yellow sand—but this blamed thing keeps rippling and flickering all the time—Ha! there's the girl herself—come into her bedroom. My! I hope she doesn't start to undress in it—that would be fearfully uncomfortable with all these people here. No, she's not undressing—she's gone and opened the cupboard. What's that she's doing—taking out a milk jug and a glass—empty, eh? I guess it must be, because she seemed to hold it upside down. Now she's picked up a sugar bowl—empty, too, eh? —and a cake tin, and that's empty—What on earth does she take them all out for if they're empty? Why can't she speak? I think—hullo—who's this coming in? Pretty hard-looking sort of woman—what's she got in her hand? — some sort of paper, I guess—she looks like a landlady, I shouldn't wonder if—

Flick, flick! Say! Look there on the screen:

"YOU OWE ME
THREE WEEKS' RENT. "

Oh, I catch on! that's what the landlady says, eh? Say! That's a mighty smart way to indicate it isn't it? I was on to that in a minute—flick, flick—hullo, the landlady's vanished—what's the girl doing now—say, she's praying! Look at her face! Doesn't she look religious, eh?

Flick, flick!

Oh, look, they've put her face, all by itself, on the screen. My! what a big face she's got when you see it like that.

She's in her room again—she's taking off her jacket—by Gee! She *is* going to bed! Here, stop the machine; it doesn't seem—Flick, flick!

Well, look at that! She's in bed, all in one flick, and fast asleep! Something must have broken in the machine and missed out a chunk. There! she's asleep all right—looks as if she was dreaming. Now it's sort of fading. I wonder how they make it do that? I guess they turn the wick of the lamp down low: that was the way in Robinson Crusoe—Flick, flick!

Hullo! where on earth is this—farmhouse, I guess—must be away upstate somewhere—who on earth are these people? Old man— white whiskers—old lady at a spinning-wheel—see it go, eh? Just like real! And a young man—that must be John Holdfast—and a girl with her hand in his. Why! Say! it's the girl, the same girl,

34

Madeline—only what's she doing away off here at this farm—how did she get clean back from the bedroom to this farm? Flick, flick! what's this?

> "NO, JOHN, I CANNOT MARRY YOU.
> I MUST DEVOTE MY LIFE
> TO MY MUSIC. "

Who says that? What music? Here, stop—

It's all gone. What's this new place? Flick, flick, looks like a street. Say! see the street car coming along—well! say! isn't that great? A street car! And here's Madeline! How on earth did she get back from the old farm all in a second? Got her street things on—that must be music under her arm—I wonder where—hullo—who's this man in a silk hat and swell coat? Gee! he's well dressed. See him roll his eyes at Madeline! He's lifting his hat—I guess he must be Edward Something, the Roo—only a roo would dress as well as he does—he's going to speak to her—

> "SIR, I DO NOT KNOW YOU.
> LET ME PASS. "

Oh, I see! The Roo mistook her; he thought she was somebody that he knew! And she wasn't! I catch on! It gets easy to understand these pictures once you're on.

Flick, flick—Oh, say, stop! I missed a piece—where is she? Outside a street door—she's pausing a moment outside—that was lucky her pausing like that—it just gave me time to read EMPLOYMENT BUREAU on the door. Gee! I read it quick.

Flick, flick! Where is it now? —oh, I see, she's gone in—she's in there—this must be the Bureau, eh? There's Madeline going up to the desk.

> "NO, WE HAVE TOLD YOU BEFORE,
> WE HAVE NOTHING... "

Pshaw! I read too slow—she's on the street again. Flick, flick!

No, she isn't—she's back in her room—cupboard still empty—no milk—no sugar—Flick, flick!

Kneeling down to pray—my! but she's religious—flick, flick—now she's on the street—got a letter in her hand—what's the address— Flick, flick!

> Mr. Meadowlark
> Meadow Farm
> Meadow County
> New York

Gee! They've put it right on the screen! The whole letter! Flick, flick—here's Madeline again on the street with the letter still in her hand—she's gone to a letter-box with it—why doesn't she post it? What's stopping her?

> "I CANNOT TELL THEM
> OF MY FAILURE.
> IT WOULD BREAK THEIR... "

Break their what? They slide these things along altogether too quick—anyway, she won't post it—I see—she's torn it up—Flick, flick!

Where is it now? Another street—seems like everything —that's a restaurant, I guess—say, it looks a swell place—see the people getting out of the motor and going in—and another lot right after them—there's Madeline —she's stopped outside the window—she's looking in—it's starting to snow! Hullo! here's a man coming along! Why, it's the Roo; he's stopping to talk to her, and pointing in at the restaurant—Flick, flick!

> "LET ME TAKE YOU IN HERE
> TO DINNER. "

Oh, I see! The Roo says that! My! I'm getting on to the scheme of these things—the Roo is going to buy her some dinner! That's decent of him. He must have heard about her being hungry up in her room—say, I'm glad he came along. Look, there's a waiter come out to the door to show them in—what! she won't go! Say! I don't understand! Didn't it say he offered to take her in? Flick, flick!

> "I WOULD RATHER DIE
> THAN EAT IT. "

Gee! Why's that? What are all the audience applauding for? I must have missed something! Flick, flick!

Oh, blazes! I'm getting lost! Where is she now? Back in her room—flick, flick—praying—flick, flick! She's out on the street! —flick, flick! —in the employment bureau —flick, flick! —out of it—flick—darn the thing! It changes too much—where is it all? What is it all—? Flick, flick!

Now it's back at the old farm—I understand that all right, anyway! Same kitchen—same old man—same old woman—she's crying—who's this? —man in a sort of uniform—oh, I see, rural postal delivery—oh, yes, he brings them their letters—I see—

> "NO, MR. MEADOWLARK,
> I AM SORRY,
> I HAVE STILL NO LETTER
> FOR YOU... "

Flick! It's gone! Flick, flick—it's Madeline's room again—what's she doing? —writing a letter? —no, she's quit writing—she's tearing it up—

> "I CANNOT WRITE.
> IT WOULD BREAK THEIR... "

Flick—missed it again! Break their something or other —Flick, flick!

Now it's the farm again—oh, yes, that's the young man John Holdfast—he's got a valise in his hand—he must be going away—they're shaking hands with him—he's saying something—

> "I WILL FIND HER FOR YOU
> IF I HAVE TO SEARCH
> ALL NEW YORK. "

He's off—there he goes through the gate—they're waving good-bye—flick—it's a railway depot—flick—it's New York—say! That's the Grand Central Depot! See the people buying tickets! My! isn't it lifelike? —and there's John—he's got here all right—I hope he finds her room—

The picture changed—where is it now? Oh, yes, I see —Madeline and the Roo—outside a street entrance to some place—he's trying to get her to come in—what's that on the door? Oh, yes, DANCE HALL—Flick, flick!

Well, say, that must be the inside of the dance hall —they're dancing—see, look, look, there's one of the girls going to get up and dance on the table.

Flick! Darn it! —they've cut it off—it's outside again —it's Madeline and the Roo—she's saying something to him—my! doesn't she look proud—?

"I WILL DIE RATHER THAN DANCE. "

Isn't she splendid! Hear the audience applaud! Flick—it's changed— it's Madeline's room again—that's the landlady —doesn't she look hard, eh? What's this—Flick!

"IF YOU CANNOT PAY, YOU MUST
LEAVE TO-NIGHT. "

Flick, flick—it's Madeline—she's out in the street—it's snowing— she's sat down on a doorstep—say, see her face, isn't if pathetic? There! They've put her face all by itself on the screen. See her eyes move! Flick, flick!

Who's this? Where is it? Oh, yes, I get it—it's John—at a police station—he's questioning them—how grave they look, eh? Flick, flick!

"HAVE YOU SEEN A GIRL
IN NEW YORK? "

I guess that's what he asks them, eh? Flick, flick—

"NO, WE HAVE NOT. "

Too bad—flick—it's changed again—it's Madeline on the doorstep— she's fallen asleep—oh, say, look at that man coming near to her on tiptoes, and peeking at her—why, it's Edward, it's the Roo—but he doesn't waken her—what does it mean? What's he after? Flick, flick—

Hullo—what's this? —it's night—what's this huge dark thing all steel, with great ropes against the sky—it's Brooklyn Bridge—at midnight—there's a woman on it! It's Madeline—see! see! She's going to jump—stop her! Stop her! Flick, flick—

Hullo! she didn't jump after all—there she is again on the doorstep—asleep—how could she jump over Brooklyn Bridge and still be asleep? I don't catch on—or, oh, yes, I do—she *dreamed* it—I see now, that's a great scheme, eh? —shows her *dream*—

The picture's changed—what's this place—a saloon, I guess—yes, there's the bartender, mixing drinks—men talking at little tables—aren't they a tough-looking lot? —see, that one's got a revolver—why, it's Edward the Roo—talking with two men—he's giving them money—what's this? —

      "GIVE US A HUNDRED APIECE
      AND WE'LL DO IT. "

It's in the street again—Edward and one of the two toughs —they've got little black masks on—they're sneaking up to Madeline where she sleeps—they've got a big motor drawn up beside them—look, they've grabbed hold of Madeline—they're lifting her into the motor—help! Stop! Aren't there any police? —yes, yes, there's a man who sees it—by Gee! It's John, John Holdfast—grab them, John—pshaw! they've jumped into the motor, they're off!

Where is it now? —oh, yes—it's the police station again —that's John, he's telling them about it—he's all out of breath—look, that head man, the big fellow, he's giving orders—

      "INSPECTOR FORDYCE, TAKE YOUR
      BIGGEST CAR AND TEN MEN.
      IF YOU OVERTAKE THEM,
      SHOOT AND SHOOT
      TO KILL. "

Hoorah! Isn't it great—hurry! don't lose a minute—see them all buckling on revolvers—get at it, boys, get at it! Don't lose a second—

Look, look—it's a motor—full speed down the street—look at the houses fly past—it's the motor with the thugs—there it goes round the corner—it's getting smaller, it's getting smaller, but look, here comes another—my! it's just flying—it's full of police—there's John in front—Flick!

Now it's the first motor—it's going over a bridge—it's heading for the country—say, isn't that car just flying —Flick, flick!

It's the second motor—it's crossing the bridge too—hurry, boys, make it go! —Flick, flick!

Out in the country—a country road—early daylight—see the wind in the trees! Notice the branches waving? Isn't it natural? —whiz! Biff! There goes the motor—biff! There goes the other one—right after it— hoorah!

The open road again—the first motor flying along! Hullo, what's wrong? It's slackened, it stops—hoorah! it's broken down—there's Madeline inside—there's Edward the Roo! Say! isn't he pale and desperate!

Hoorah! the police! the police! all ten of them in their big car—see them jumping out—see them pile into the thugs! Down with them! paste their heads off! Shoot them! Kill them! isn't it great—isn't it educative—that's the Roo—Edward—with John at his throat! Choke him, John! Throttle him! Hullo, it's changed—they're in the big motor—that's the Roo with the handcuffs on him.

That's Madeline—she's unbound and she's talking; say, isn't she just real pretty when she smiles?

> "YES, JOHN, I HAVE LEARNED THAT
> I WAS WRONG TO PUT MY ART
> BEFORE YOUR LOVE. I WILL
> MARRY YOU AS SOON AS
> YOU LIKE. "

Flick, flick!

What pretty music! Ding! Dong! Ding! Dong! Isn't it soft and sweet! —like wedding bells. Oh, I see, the man in the orchestra's doing it with a little triangle and a stick—it's a little church up in the country—see all the people lined up—oh! there's Madeline! in a long white veil—isn't she just sweet! —and John—

Flick, flack, flick, flack.

"BULGARIAN TROOPS ON THE
MARCH. "

What! Isn't it over? Do they all go to Bulgaria? I don't seem to understand. Anyway, I guess it's all right to go now. Other people are going.

V. The Call of the Carburettor, or,
Mr. Blinks and his Friends

"First get a motor in your own eye and then you will overlook more easily the motor in your brother's eye. " —Somewhere in the Bible.

"By all means let's have a reception, " said Mrs. Blinks. "It's the quickest and nicest way to meet our old friends again after all these years. And goodness knows this house is big enough for it"—she gave a glance as she spoke round the big reception-room of the Blinkses' residence—"and these servants seem to understand things so perfectly it's no trouble to us to give anything. Only don't let's ask a whole lot of chattering young people that we don't know; let's have the older people, the ones that can talk about something really worth while. "

"That's just what I say, " answered Mr. Blinks—he was a small man with insignificance written all over him—"let me listen to people talk; that's what *I* like. I'm not much on the social side myself, but I do enjoy hearing good talk. That's what I liked so much over in England. All them—all those people that we used to meet talked so well. And in France those ladies that run saloons on Sunday afternoons—"

"Sallongs, " corrected Mrs. Blinks. "It's sounded like it was a G. " She picked up a pencil and paper. "Well, then, " she said, as she began to write down names, "we'll ask Judge Ponderus—"

"Sure! " assented Mr. Blinks, rubbing his hands. "He's a fine talker, if he'll come! "

"They'll all come, " said his wife, "to a house as big as this; and we'll ask the Rev. Dr. Domb and his wife—or, no, he's Archdeacon Domb now, I hear—and he'll invite Bishop Sollem, so they can talk together."

"That'll be good, " said Mr. Blinks. "I remember years and years ago hearing them two—those two, talking about religion, all about the soul and the body. Man! It was deep. It was clean beyond me. That's what I like to listen to. "

"And Professor Potofax from the college, " went on Mrs. Blinks. "You remember, the big stout one. "

"I know, " said her husband.

"And his daughter, she's musical, and Mrs. Buncomtalk, she's a great light on woman suffrage, and Miss Scragg and Mr. Underdone—they both write poetry, so they can talk about that. "

"It'll be a great treat to listen to them all, " said Mr. Blinks.

A week later, on the day of the Blinkses' reception, there was a string of motors three deep along a line of a hundred yards in front of the house.

Inside the reception rooms were filled.

Mr. Blinks, insignificant even in his own house, moved to and fro among his guests.

Archdeacon Domb and Dean Sollem were standing side by side with their heads gravely lowered, as they talked, over the cups of tea that they held in their hands.

Mr. Blinks edged towards them.

"This'll be something pretty good, " he murmured to himself as he got within reach of their conversation.

"What do you do about your body? " the Archdeacon was asking in his deep, solemn tones.

"Practically nothing, " said the Bishop. "A little rub of shellac now and then, but practically nothing. "

"You wash it, of course? " asked Dr. Domb.

"Only now and again, but far less than you would think. I really take very little thought for my body. "

"Ah, " said Dr. Domb reflectively, "I went all over mine last summer with linseed oil. "

"Framed" format; resembles screenplay

"But didn't you find, " said the Bishop, "that it got into your pipes and choked your feed? "

"It did, " said Dr. Domb, munching a bit of toast as he spoke. "In fact, I have had a lot of trouble with my feed ever since. "

"Try flushing your pipes out with hot steam, " said the Bishop. Mr. Blinks had listened in something like dismay.

"Motor-cars! " he murmured. "Who'd have thought it? "

But at this moment a genial, hearty-looking person came pushing towards him with a cheery greeting.

"I'm afraid I'm rather late, Blinks, " he said.

"Delayed in court, eh. Judge? " said Blinks as he shook hands.

"No, blew out a plug! " said the Judge. "Stalled me right up. "

"Blew out a plug! " exclaimed Dr. Domb and the Bishop, deeply interested at once.

"A cracked insulator, I think, " said the Judge.

"Possibly, " said the Archdeacon very gravely, "the terminal nuts of your dry battery were loose. "

Mr. Blinks moved slowly away.

"Dear me! " he mused, "how changed they are. "

It was a relief to him to edge his way quietly into another group of guests where he felt certain that the talk would be of quite another kind.

Professor Potofax and Miss Scragg and a number of others were evidently talking about books.

"A beautiful book, " the professor was saying. "One of the best things, to my mind at any rate, that has appeared for years. There's a chapter on the silencing of exhaust gas which is simply marvellous. "

"Is it illustrated? " questioned one of the ladies.

"Splendidly, " said the professor. "Among other things there are sectional views of check valves and flexible roller bearings—"

"Ah, do tell me about the flexible bearings, " murmured Miss Scragg.

Mr. Blinks moved on.

Wherever he went among his guests, they all seemed stricken with the same mania. He caught their conversation in little scraps.

"I ran her up to forty with the greatest of ease, then threw in my high speed and got seventy out of her without any trouble. "—"No, I simply used a socket wrench, it answers perfectly. "—"Yes, a solution of calcium chloride is very good, but of course the hydrochloric acid in it has a powerful effect on the metal. "

"Dear me, " mused Mr. Blinks, "are they all mad? "

Meantime, around his wife, who stood receiving in state at one end of the room, the guests surged to and fro.

"So charmed to see you again, " exclaimed one. "You've been in Europe a long time, haven't you? Oh, mostly in the south of England? Are the roads good? Last year my husband and I went all through Shakespeare's country. It's just delightful. They sprinkle it so thoroughly. And Stratford-on-Avon itself is just a treat. It's all oiled, every bit of it, except the little road by Shakespeare's house; but we didn't go along that. Then later we went up to the lake district: but it's not so good: they don't oil it. "

She floated away, to give place to another lady.

"In France every summer? " she exclaimed. "Oh, how perfectly lovely. Don't you think the French cars simply divine? My husband thinks the French body is far better modelled than ours. He saw ever so many of them. He thought of bringing one over with him, but it costs such a lot to keep them in good order. "

"The theatres? " said another lady. "How you must have enjoyed them. I just love the theatres. Last week my husband and I were at the *Palatial*—it's moving pictures—where they have that film with the motor collision running. It's just wonderful. You see the motors going at full speed, and then smash right into one another — and all the people killed — it's really fine. "

"Have they all gone insane? " said Mr. Blinks to his wife after the guests had gone.

"Dreadful, isn't it? " she assented. "I never was so bored in my life. "

"Why, they talk of nothing else but their motor-cars! " said Blinks. "We've got to get a car, I suppose, living at this distance from the town, but I'm hanged if I intend to go clean crazy over it like these people. "

And the guests as they went home talked of the Blinkses.

"I fear, " said Dr. Domb to Judge Ponderus, "that Blinks has hardly profited by his time in Europe as much as he ought to have. He seems to have observed *nothing*. I was asking him about the new Italian touring car that they are using so much in Rome. He said he had never noticed it. And he was there a month! "

"Is it possible? " said the Judge. "Where were his eyes? "

All of which showed that Mr. and Mrs. Blinks were in danger of losing their friends for ever.

But it so happened that about three weeks later Blinks came home to his residence in an obvious state of excitement. His face was flushed and he had on a silly little round cap with a glazed peak.

"Why, Clarence, " cried his wife, "whatever is the matter? "

"Matter! " he exclaimed. "There isn't anything the matter! I bought a car this morning, that's all. Say, it's a beauty, a regular peach, four thousand with ten off. I ran it clean round the shed alone first time. The chauffeur says he never saw anybody get on to the hang of it so quick. Get on your hat and come right down to the garage. I've got a man waiting there to teach you to run it. Hurry up! "

Within a week or two after that one might see the Blinkses any morning, in fact every morning, out in their car!

"Good morning, Judge! " calls Blinks gaily as he passes, "how's that carburettor acting? —Good morning. Archdeacon, is that plug trouble of yours all right again? —Hullo, Professor, let me pick you up and ride you up to the college; oh, it's no trouble. What do you think of the bearings of this car? Aren't they just dandy? "

And so Mr. Blinks has got all his friends back again.

After all, the great thing about being crazy is to be all crazy together.

VI. The Two Sexes in Fives or Sixes.
A Dinner-party Study

"But, surely, " exclaimed the Hostess, looking defiantly and searchingly through the cut flowers of the centre-piece, so that her eye could intimidate in turn all the five men at the table, "one must admit that women are men's equals in every way? "

The Lady-with-the-Bust tossed her head a little and echoed, "Oh, surely! "

The Debutante lifted her big blue eyes a little towards the ceiling, with the upward glance that stands for innocence. She said nothing, waiting for a cue as to what to appear to be.

Meantime the Chief Lady Guest, known to be in suffrage work, was pinching up her lips and getting her phrases ready, like a harpooner waiting to strike. She knew that the Hostess meant this as an opening for her.

But the Soft Lady Whom Men Like toyed with a bit of bread on the tablecloth (she had a beautiful hand) and smiled gently. The other women would have called it a simper. To the men it stood for profound intelligence.

The five men that sat amongst and between the ladies received the challenge of the Hostess's speech and answered it each in his own way.

From the Heavy Host at the head of the table there came a kind of deep grunt, nothing more. He had heard this same talk at each of his dinners that season.

There was a similar grunt from the Heavy Business Friend of the Host, almost as broad and thick as the Host himself. He knew too what was coming. He proposed to stand by his friend, man for man. He could sympathise. The Lady-with-the-Bust was his wife.

But the Half Man with the Moon Face, who was known to work side by side with women on committees and who called them "Comrades, " echoed:

"Oh, surely! " with deep emphasis.

The Smooth Gentleman, there for business reasons, exclaimed with great alacrity, "Women equal! Oh, rather! "

Last of all the Interesting Man with Long Hair, known to write for the magazines—all of them—began at once:

"I remember once saying to Mrs. Pankhurst—" but was overwhelmed in the general conversation before he could say what it was he remembered saying to Mrs. Pankhurst.

In other words, the dinner-party, at about course number seven, had reached the inevitable moment of the discussion of the two sexes.

It had begun as dinner-parties do.

Everybody had talked gloomily to his neighbour, over the oysters, on one drink of white wine; more or less brightly to two people, over the fish, on two drinks; quite brilliantly to three people on three drinks; and then the conversation had become general and the European war had been fought through three courses with champagne. Everybody had taken an extremely broad point of view. The Heavy Business Friend had declared himself absolutely impartial and had at once got wet with rage over cotton. The Chief Lady Guest had explained that she herself was half English on her mother's side, and the Lady-with- the-Bust had told how a lady friend of hers had a cousin who had travelled in Hungary. She admitted that it was some years ago. Things might have changed since. Then the Interesting Man, having got the table where he wanted it, had said: "I remember when I was last in Sofia—by the way it is pronounced Say-ah-fee-ah—talking with Radovitch—or Radee-ah-vitch, as it should be sounded—the foreign secretary, on what the Sobranje—it is pronounced Soophrangee—would be likely to do"—and by the time he had done with the Sobranje no one dared speak of the war any more.

But the Hostess had got out of it the opening she wanted, and she said:

"At any rate, it is wonderful what women have done in the war—"

"And are doing, " echoed the Half Man with the Moon Face.

And then it was that the Hostess had said that surely every one must admit women are equal to men and the topic of the sexes was started. All the women had been waiting for it, anyway. It is the only topic that women care about. Even men can stand it provided that fifty per cent or more of the women present are handsome enough to justify it.

"I hardly see how, after all that has happened, any rational person could deny for a moment, " continued the Hostess, looking straight at her husband and his Heavy Business Friend, "that women are equal and even superior to men. Surely our brains are just as good? " and she gave an almost bitter laugh.

"Don't you think perhaps—? " began the Smooth Gentleman.

"No, I don't, " said the Hostess. "You're going to say that we are inferior in things like mathematics or in logical reasoning. We are not. But, after all, the only reason why we are is because of training. Think of the thousands of years that men have been trained. Answer me that? "

"Well, might it not be—? " began the Smooth Gentleman.

"I don't think so for a moment, " said the Hostess. "I think if we'd only been trained as men have for the last two or three thousand years our brains would be just as well trained for the things they were trained for as they would have been now for the things we have been trained for and in that case wouldn't have. Don't you agree with me, " she said, turning to the Chief Lady Guest, whom she suddenly remembered, "that, after all, we think more clearly? "

Here the Interesting Man, who had been silent longer than an Interesting Man can, without apoplexy, began:

"I remember once saying in London to Sir Charles Doosey—"

But the Chief Lady Guest refused to be checked.

"We've been gathering some rather interesting statistics, " she said, speaking very firmly, syllable by syllable, "on that point at our Settlement. We have measured the heads of five hundred factory girls, making a chart of them, you know, and the feet of five hundred domestic servants—"

"And don't you find—" began the Smooth Gentleman.

"No, " said the Chief Lady Guest firmly, "we do not. But I was going to say that when we take our measurements and reduce them to a scale of a hundred—I think you understand me—"

"Ah, but come, now, " interrupted the Interesting man, "there's nothing really more deceitful than anthropometric measures. I remember once saying (in London) to Sir Robert Bittell—*the* Sir Robert Bittell, you know—"

Here everybody murmured, "Oh, yes, " except the Heavy Host and his Heavy Friend, who with all their sins were honest men.

"I said, 'Sir Robert, I want your frank opinion, your very frank opinion—'"

But here there was a slight interruption. The Soft Lady accidentally dropped a bangle from her wrist on to the floor. Now all through the dinner she had hardly said anything, but she had listened for twenty minutes (from the grapefruit to the fish) while the Interesting Man had told her about his life in Honduras (it is pronounced Hondooras), and for another twenty while the Smooth Gentleman, who was a barrister, had discussed himself as a pleader. And when each of the men had begun to speak in the general conversation, she had looked deep into their faces as if hanging on to their words. So when she dropped her bangle two of the men leaped from their chairs to get it, and the other three made a sort of struggle as they sat. By the time it was recovered and replaced upon her arm (a very beautiful arm), the Interesting Man was side-tracked and the Chief Lady Guest, who had gone on talking during the bangle hunt, was heard saying:

"Entirely so. That seems to me the greatest difficulty before us. So few men are willing to deal with the question with perfect sincerity."

She laid emphasis on the word and the Half Man with the Moon Face took his cue from it and threw a pose of almost painful sincerity.

"Why is it, " continued the Chief Lady Guest, "that men always insist on dealing with us just as if we were playthings, just so many dressed-up dolls? "

Here the Debutante immediately did a doll.

"If a woman is attractive and beautiful, " the lady went on, "so much the better. " (She had no intention of letting go of the doll business entirely.) "But surely you men ought to value us as something more than mere dolls? "

She might have pursued the topic, but at this moment the Smooth Gentleman, who made a rule of standing in all round, and had broken into a side conversation with the Silent Host, was overheard to say something about women's sense of humour.

The table was in a turmoil in a moment, three of the ladies speaking at once. To deny a woman's sense of humour is the last form of social insult.

"I entirely disagree with you, " said the Chief Lady Guest, speaking very severely. "I know it from my own case, from my own sense of humour and from observation. Last week, for example, we measured no less than seventy-five factory girls—"

"Well, I'm sure, " said the Lady-with-the-Bust, "I don't know what men mean by our not having a sense of humour. I'm sure I have. I know I went last week to a vaudeville, and I just laughed all through. Of course I can't read Mark Twain, or anything like that, but then I don't call that funny, do you? " she concluded, turning to the Hostess.

But the Hostess, feeling somehow that the ground was dangerous, had already risen, and in a moment more the ladies had floated out of the room and upstairs to the drawing-room, where they spread themselves about in easy chairs in billows of pretty coloured silk.

"How charming it is, " the Chief Lady Guest began, "to find men coming so entirely to our point of view! Do you know it was so delightful to-night: I hardly heard a word of dissent or contradiction."

Thus they talked; except the Soft Lady, who had slipped into a seat by herself with an album over her knees, and with an empty chair on either side of her. There she waited.

Meantime, down below, the men had shifted into chairs to one end of the table and the Heavy Host was shoving cigars at them, thick as ropes, and passing the port wine, with his big fist round the neck of the decanter. But for his success in life he could have had a place as a bar tender anywhere.

None of them spoke till the cigars were well alight.

Then the Host said very deliberately, taking each word at his leisure, with smoke in between:

"Of course—this—suffrage business—"

"Tommyrot! " exclaimed the Smooth Gentleman, with great alacrity, his mask entirely laid aside.

"Damn foolishness, " gurgled the Heavy Business Friend, sipping his port.

"Of course you can't really discuss it with women, " murmured the Host.

"Oh, no, " assented all the others. Even the Half Man sipped his wine and turned traitor, there being no one to see.

"You see, " said the Host, "if my wife likes to go to meetings and be on committees, why, I don't stop her. "

"Neither do I mine, " said the Heavy Friend. "It amuses her, so I let her do it. " His wife, the Lady-with-the-Bust, was safely out of hearing.

"I remember once, " began the Interesting Man, "saying to"—he paused a moment, for the others were looking at him—"another man that if women did get the vote they'd never use it, anyway. All they like is being talked about for not getting it. "

After which, having exhausted the Woman Question, the five men turned to such bigger subjects as the fall in sterling exchange and the President's seventeenth note to Germany.

Then presently they went upstairs. And when they reached the door of the drawing-room a keen observer, or, indeed, any kind of observer, might have seen that all five of them made an obvious advance towards the two empty seats beside the Soft Lady.

VII. The Grass Bachelor's Guide.
With sincere Apologies to the Ladies' Periodicals

There are periods in the life of every married man when he is turned for the time being into a grass bachelor.

This happens, for instance, in the summer time when his wife is summering by the sea, and he himself is simmering in the city. It happens also in the autumn when his wife is in Virginia playing golf in order to restore her shattered nerves after the fatigues of the seaside. It occurs again in November when his wife is in the Adirondacks to get the benefit of the altitude, and later on through the winter when she is down in Florida to get the benefit of the latitude. The breaking up of the winter being, notoriously, a trying time on the system, any reasonable man is apt to consent to his wife's going to California. In the later spring, the season of the bursting flowers and the young buds, every woman likes to be with her mother in the country. It is not fair to stop her.

It thus happens that at various times of the year a great number of men, unable to leave their business, are left to their own resources as housekeepers in their deserted houses and apartments. It is for their benefit that I have put together these hints on housekeeping for men. It may be that in composing them I owe something to the current number of the leading women's magazines. If so, I need not apologise. I am sure that in these days We Men all feel that We Men and We Women are so much alike, or at least those of us who call ourselves so, that we need feel no jealousy when We Men and We Women are striving each, or both, in the same direction if in opposite ways. I hope that I make myself clear. I am sure I do.

So I feel that if We Men, who are left alone in our houses and apartments in the summer-time, would only set ourselves to it, we could make life not only a little brighter for ourselves but also a little less bright for those about us.

Nothing contributes to this end so much as good housekeeping. The first thing for the housekeeper to realise is that it is impossible for him to attend to his housekeeping in the stiff and unbecoming garments of his business hours. When he begins his day he must therefore carefully consider—

WHAT TO WEAR BEFORE DRESSING

The simplest and best thing will be found to be a plain sacque or kimono, cut very full so as to allow of the freest movement, and buttoned either down the front or back or both. If the sleeve is cut short at the elbow and ruffled above the bare arm, the effect is both serviceable and becoming. It will be better, especially for such work as lighting the gas range and boiling water, to girdle the kimono with a simple yet effective rope or tasselled silk, which may be drawn in or let out according to the amount of water one wishes to boil. A simple kimono of this sort can be bought almost anywhere for $2.50, or can be supplied by Messrs. Einstein & Fickelbrot (see advertising pages) for twenty-five dollars.

Having a kimono such as this, our housekeeper can either button himself into it with a button-hook (very good ones are supplied by Messrs. Einstein & Fickelbrot [see ad.] at a very reasonable price or even higher), or better still, he can summon the janitor of the apartment, who can button him up quite securely in a few minutes' time —a quarter of an hour at the most. We Men cannot impress upon ourselves too strongly that, for efficient housekeeping, time is everything, and that much depends on quiet, effective movement from place to place, or from any one place to any number of other places. We are now ready to consider the all-important question—

WHAT TO SELECT FOR BREAKFAST

Our housekeeper will naturally desire something that is simple and easily cooked, yet at the same time sustaining and invigorating and containing a maximum of food value with a minimum of cost. If he is wise he will realise that the food ought to contain a proper quantity of both proteids and amygdaloids, and, while avoiding a nitrogenous breakfast, should see to it that he obtains sufficient of what is albuminous and exogamous to prevent his breakfast from becoming monotonous. Careful thought must therefore be given to the breakfast menu.

For the purpose of thinking, a simple but very effective costume may be devised by throwing over the kimono itself a thin lace shawl, with a fichu carried high above the waistline and terminating in a plain insertion. A bit of old lace thrown over the housekeeper's head is at once serviceable and becoming and will help to keep the dust out of his brain while thinking what to eat for breakfast.

Very naturally our housekeeper's first choice will be some kind of cereal. The simplest and most economical breakfast of this kind can be secured by selecting some cereal or grain food—such as oats, flax, split peas that have been carefully strained in the colander, or beans that have been fired off in a gun. Any of these cereals may be bought for ten cents a pound at a grocer's—or obtained from Messrs. Einstein & Fickelbrot for a dollar a pound, or more. Supposing then that we have decided upon a pound of split peas as our breakfast, the next task that devolves upon our housekeeper is to—

GO OUT AND BUY IT

Here our advice is simple but positive. Shopping should never be done over the telephone or by telegraph. The good housekeeper instead of telegraphing for his food will insist on seeing his food himself, and will eat nothing that he does not first see before eating. This is a cardinal rule. For the moment, then, the range must be turned low while our housekeeper sallies forth to devote himself to his breakfast shopping. The best costume for shopping is a simple but effective suit, cut in plain lines, either square or crosswise, and buttoned wherever there are button-holes. A simple hat of some dark material may be worn together with plain boots drawn up well over the socks and either laced or left unlaced. No harm is done if a touch of colour is added by carrying a geranium in the hand. We are now ready for the street.

TEST OF EFFECTIVE SHOPPING

Here we may say at once that the crucial test is that we must know what we want, why we want it, where we want it, and what it is. Time, as We Men are only too apt to forget, is everything, and since our aim is now a pound of split peas we must, as we sally forth, think of a pound of split peas and only a pound. A cheery salutation may be exchanged with other morning shoppers as we pass along, but only exchanged. Split peas being for the moment our prime business, we must, as rapidly and unobtrusively as possible, visit those shops and only those shops where split peas are to be had.

Having found the split peas, our housekeeper's next task is to *pay* for them. This he does with money that may be either carried in the hand or, better, tucked into a simple *etui*, or *dodu*, that can be carried at the wrist or tied to the ankle. The order duly given, our housekeeper gives his address for the delivery of the peas, and then, as quietly and harmlessly as possible, returns to his apartment. His next office, and a most important one it is, is now ready to be performed. This new but necessary duty is—

WAITING FOR THE DELIVERY VAN

A good costume for waiting for the delivery van in, is a simple brown suit, slashed with yellow and purple, and sliced or gored from the hip to the feet. As time is everything, the housekeeper, after having put on his slashed costume for waiting for the delivery van, may set himself to the performance of a number of light household tasks, at the same time looking occasionally from the window so as to detect the arrival of the van as soon as possible after it has arrived. Among other things, he may now feed his canary by opening its mouth with a button-hook and dropping in coffee beans till the little songster shows by its gratified air that it is full. A little time may be well spent among the flowers and bulbs of the apartment, clipping here a leaf and here a stem, and removing the young buds and bugs. For work among the flowers, a light pair of rather long scissors, say a foot long, can be carried at the girdle, or attached to the *etui* and passed over the shoulder with a looped cord so as to fall in an easy and graceful fold across the back. The moment is now approaching when we may expect—

THE ARRIVAL OF THE VAN

The housekeeper will presently discover the van, drawn up in the front of the apartment, and its driver curled up on the seat. Now is the moment of activity. Hastily throwing on a *peignoir*, the housekeeper descends and, receiving his parcel, reascends to his apartment. The whole descent and reascent is made quickly, quietly, and, if possible, only once.

PUTTING THE PEAS TO SOAK

Remember that unsoaked peas are hard, forcible, and surcharged with a nitrogenous amygdaloid that is in reality what chemical science calls putrate of lead. On the other hand, peas that are soaked become large, voluble, textile, and, while extremely palatable, are none the less rich in glycerine, starch, and other lacteroids and bactifera. To contain the required elements of nutrition split peas must be soaked for two hours in fresh water and afterwards boiled for an hour and a quarter (eighty-five minutes).

It is now but the work of a moment to lift the saucepan of peas from the fire, strain them through a colander, pass them thence into a net or bag, rinse them in cold water and then spread the whole appetising mass on a platter and carry it on a fireshovel to the dining-room. As it is now about six o'clock in the evening, our housekeeper can either—

TELEPHONE TO HIS CLUB
AND ORDER A THIN SOUP
WITH A BITE OF FISH,
TWO LAMB CHOPS WITH ASPARAGUS,
AND SEND WORD ALSO
FOR A PINT OF MOSELLE
TO BE LAID ON ICE

Or he can sit down and eat those d—n peas.

WE KNOW WHICH HE WILL DO

VIII. Every Man and his Friends. Mr. Crunch's Portrait Gallery (as Edited from his Private Thoughts)

(I) HIS VIEWS ON HIS EMPLOYER

A mean man. I say it, of course, without any prejudice, and without the slightest malice. But the man is mean. Small, I think, is the word. I am not thinking, of course, of my own salary. It is not a matter that I would care to refer to; though, as a matter of fact, one would think that after fifteen years of work an application for an increase of five hundred dollars is the kind of thing that any man ought to be glad to meet half-way. Not that I bear the man any malice for it. None. If he died to-morrow, no one would regret his death as genuinely as I would: if he fell into the river and got drowned, or if he fell into a sewer and suffocated, or if he got burned to death in a gas explosion (there are a lot of things that might happen to him), I should feel genuinely sorry to see him cut off.

But what strikes me more than the man's smallness is his incompetence. The man is absolutely no good. It's not a thing that I would say outside: as a matter of fact I deny it every time I hear it, though every man in town knows it. How that man ever got the position he has is more than I can tell. And, as for holding it, he couldn't hold it half a day if it weren't that the rest of us in the office do practically everything for him.

Why, I've seen him send out letters (I wouldn't say this to anyone outside, of course, and I wouldn't like to have it repeated)—letters with, actually, mistakes in English. Think of it, in English! Ask his stenographer.

I often wonder why I go on working for him. There are dozens of other companies that would give anything to get me. Only the other day—it's not ten years ago—I had an offer, or practically an offer, to go to Japan selling Bibles. I often wish now I had taken it. I believe I'd like the Japanese. They're gentlemen, the Japanese. They wouldn't turn a man down after slaving away for fifteen years.

I often think I'll quit him. I say to my wife that that man had better not provoke me too far; or some day I'll just step into his office and tell him exactly what I think of him. I'd like to. I often say it over to myself in the street car coming home.

He'd better be careful, that's all.

(II) THE MINISTER WHOSE CHURCH HE ATTENDS

A dull man. Dull is the only word I can think of that exactly describes him—dull and prosy. I don't say that he is not a good man. He may be. I don't say that he is not. I have never seen any sign of it, if he is. But I make it a rule never to say anything to take away a man's character.

And his sermons! Really that sermon he gave last Sunday on Esau seemed to me the absolute limit. I wish you could have heard it. I mean to say—drivel. I said to my wife and some friends, as we walked away from the church, that a sermon like that seemed to me to come from the dregs of the human intellect. Mind you, I don't believe in criticising a sermon. I always feel it a sacred obligation never to offer a word of criticism. When I say that the sermon was *punk,* I don't say it as criticism. I merely state it as a fact. And to think that we pay that man eighteen hundred dollars a year! And he's in debt all the time at that. What does he do with it? He can't spend it. It's not as if he had a large family (they've only four children). It's just a case of sheer extravagance. He runs about all the time. Last year it was a trip to a Synod Meeting at New York—away four whole days; and two years before that, dashing off to a Scripture Conference at Boston, and away nearly a whole week, and his wife with him!

What I say is that if a man's going to spend his time gadding about the country like that—here to-day and there to-morrow—how on earth can he attend to his parochial duties?

I'm a religious man. At least I trust I am. I believe —and more and more as I get older—in eternal punishment. I see the need of it when I look about me. As I say, I trust I am a religious man, but when it comes to subscribing fifty dollars as they want us to, to get the man out of debt, I say "No. "

True religion, as I see it, is not connected with money.

(III) HIS PARTNER AT BRIDGE

The man is a complete ass. How a man like that has the nerve to sit down at a bridge table, I don't know. I wouldn't mind if the man had any idea—even the faintest idea—of how to play. But he hasn't any. Three times I signalled to him to throw the lead into my hand and he wouldn't: I knew that our only ghost of a chance was to let me do all the playing. But the ass couldn't see it. He even had the supreme nerve to ask me what I meant by leading diamonds when he had signalled that he had none. I couldn't help asking him, as politely as I could, why he had disregarded my signal for spades. He had the gall to ask in reply why I had overlooked his signal for clubs in the second hand round; the very time, mind you, when I had led a three spot as a sign to him to let me play the whole game. I couldn't help saying to him, at the end of the evening, in a tone of such evident satire that anyone but an ass would have recognised it, that I had seldom had as keen an evening at cards.

But he didn't see it. The irony of it was lost on him. The jackass merely said—quite amiably and unconsciously —that he thought I'd play a good game presently. Me! Play a good game presently!

I gave him a look, just one look as I went out! But I don't think he saw it. He was talking to some one else.

(IV) HIS HOSTESS AT DINNER

On what principle that woman makes up her dinner parties is more than human brain can devise. Mind you, I like going out to dinner. To my mind it's the very best form of social entertainment. But I like to find myself among people that can talk, not among a pack of numbskulls. What I like is good general conversation, about things worth talking about. But among a crowd of idiots like that what can you expect? You'd think that even society people would be interested, or pretend to be, in real things. But not a bit. I had hardly started to talk about the rate of exchange on the German mark in relation to the fall of sterling bills—a thing that you would think a whole table full of people would be glad to listen to—when first thing I knew the whole lot of them had ceased paying any attention and were listening to an insufferable ass of an Englishman—I forget his name. You'd hardly suppose that just because a man has been in Flanders and has his arm in a sling and has to have his food cut up by the butler, that's any reason for having a whole table full of people listening to him. And especially the women: they have a way of listening to a fool like that with their elbows on the table that is positively sickening.

I felt that the whole thing was out of taste and tried in vain, in one of the pauses, to give a lead to my hostess by referring to the prospect of a shipping subsidy bill going through to offset the register of alien ships. But she was too utterly dense to take it up. She never even turned her head. All through dinner that ass talked —he and that silly young actor they're always asking there that is perpetually doing imitations of the vaudeville people. That kind of thing may be all right, for those who care for it—I frankly don't—outside a theatre. But to my mind the idea of trying to throw people into fits of laughter at a dinner-table is simply execrable taste. I cannot see the sense of people shrieking with laughter at dinner. I have, I suppose, a better sense of humour than most people. But to my mind a humourous story should be told quietly and slowly in a way to bring out the point of the humour and to make it quite clear by preparing for it with proper explanations. But with people like that I find I no sooner get well started with a story than some fool or other breaks in. I had a most amusing experience the other day—that is, about fifteen years ago—at a summer hotel in the Adirondacks, that one would think would have amused even a shallow lot of people like those, but I had no sooner started to tell it—or had hardly done more than to describe the Adirondacks in a general way—than, first thing I know, my hostess, stupid woman, had risen and all the ladies were trooping out.

As to getting in a word edgeways with the men over the cigars— perfectly impossible! They're worse than the women. They were all buzzing round the infernal Englishman with questions about Flanders and the army at the front. I tried in vain to get their attention for a minute to give them my impressions of the Belgian peasantry (during my visit there in 1885), but my host simply turned to me for a second and said, "Have some more port? " and was back again listening to the asinine Englishman.

And when we went upstairs to the drawing-room I found myself, to my disgust, side-tracked in a corner of the room with that supreme old jackass of a professor—their uncle, I think, or something of the sort. In all my life I never met a prosier man. He bored me blue with long accounts of his visit to Serbia and his impressions of the Serbian peasantry in 1875.

I should have left early, but it would have been too noticeable.

The trouble with a woman like that is that she asks the wrong people to her parties.

BUT,

(V) HIS LITTLE SON

You haven't seen him? Why, that's incredible. You must have. He goes past your house every day on his way to his kindergarten. You must have seen him a thousand times. And he's a boy you couldn't help noticing. You'd pick that boy out among a hundred, right away. "There's a remarkable boy, " you'd say. I notice people always turn and look at him on the street. He's just the image of me. Everybody notices it at once.

How old? He's twelve. Twelve and two weeks yesterday. But he's so bright you'd think he was fifteen. And the things he says! You'd laugh! I've written a lot of them down in a book for fear of losing them. Some day when you come up to the house I'll read them to you. Come some evening. Come early so that we'll have lots of time. He said to me one day, "Dad" (he always calls me Dad), "what makes the sky blue? " Pretty thoughtful, eh, for a little fellow of twelve? He's always asking questions like that. I wish I could remember half of them.

And I'm bringing him up right, I tell you. I got him a little savings box a while ago, and have got him taught to put all his money in it, and not give any of it away, so that when he grows up he'll be all right.

On his last birthday I put a five dollar gold piece into it for him and explained to him what five dollars meant, and what a lot you could do with it if you hung on to it. You ought to have seen him listen.

"Dad, " he says, "I guess you're the kindest man in the world, aren't you? "
Come up some time and see him.

IX. More than Twice-told Tales; or,
Every Man his Own Hero

(I)

The familiar story told about himself by the Commercial Traveller who sold goods to the man who was regarded as impossible.

"What, " they said, "you're getting off at Midgeville? You're going to give the Jones Hardware Company a try, eh? " —and then they all started laughing and giving me the merry ha! ha! Well, I just got my grip packed and didn't say a thing and when the train slowed up for Midgeville, out I slid. "Give my love to old man Jones, " one of the boys called after me, "and get yourself a couple of porous plasters and a pair of splints before you tackle him! " —and then they all gave me the ha! ha! again, out of the window as the train pulled out.

Well, I walked uptown from the station to the Jones Hardware Company. "Is Mr. Jones in the office? " I asked of one of the young fellers behind the counter. "He's in the office, " he says, "all right, but I guess you can't see him, " he says—and he looked at my grip. "What name shall I say? " says he. "Don't say any name at all, " I says. "Just open the door and let me in. "

Well, there was old man Jones sitting scowling over his desk, biting his pen in that way he has. He looked up when I came in. "See here, young man, " he says, "you can't sell me any hardware, " he says. "Mr. Jones, " I says, "I don't *want* to sell you any hardware. I'm not *here* to sell you any hardware. I know, " I says, "as well as you do, " I says, "that I couldn't sell any hardware if I tried to. But, " I says, "I guess it don't do any harm to open up this sample case, and show you some hardware, " I says. "Young man, " says he, "if you start opening up that sample case in here, you'll lose your time, that's all" —and he turned off sort of sideways and began looking over some letters.

"That's *all right*, Mr. Jones, " I says. "That's *all right*. I'm *here* to lose my time. But I'm not going out of this room till you take a look anyway at some of this new cutlery I'm carrying. "

So open I throws my sample case right across the end of his desk. "Look at that knife, " I says, "Mr. Jones. Just look at it: clear Sheffield at three-thirty the dozen and they're a knife that will last till you wear the haft off it. " "Oh, pshaw, " he growled, "I don't want no knives; there's nothing in knives—"

Well I *knew* he didn't want knives, see? I *knew* it. But the way I opened up the sample case it showed up, just by accident so to speak, a box of those new electric burners—adjustable, you know— they'll take heat off any size of socket you like and use it for any mortal thing in the house. I saw old Jones had his eyes on them in a minute. "What's those things you got there? " he growls, "those in the box? " "Oh, " I said, "that's just a new line, " I said, "the boss wanted me to take along: some sort of electric rig for heating, " I said, "but I don't think there's anything to it. But here, now, Mr. Jones, is a spoon I've got on this trip—it's the new Delphide —you can't tell that, sir, from silver. No, sir, " I says, "I defy any man, money down, to tell that there Delphide from genuine refined silver, and they're a spoon that'll last—"

"Let me see one of those burners, " says old man Jones, breaking in.

Well, sir, in about two minutes more, I had one of the burners fixed on to the light socket, and old Jones, with his coat off, boiling water in a tin cup (out of the store) and timing it with his watch.

The next day I pulled into Toledo and went and joined the other boys up to the Jefferson House. "Well, " they says, "have you got that plaster on? " and started in to give me the ha! ha! again. "Oh, I don't know, " I says. "I guess *this* is some plaster, isn't it? " and I took out of my pocket an order from old man Jones for two thousand adjustable burners, at four-twenty with two off. "Some plaster, eh? " I says.

Well, sir, the boys looked sick.

Old man Jones gets all his stuff from our house now. Oh, he ain't bad at all when you get to know him.

(II)

The well-known story told by the man who has once had a strange psychic experience.
... What you say about presentiments reminds me of a strange experience that I had myself.

I was sitting by myself one night very late, reading. I don't remember just what it was that I was reading. I think it was—or no, I don't remember *what* it was. Well, anyway, I was sitting up late reading quietly till it got pretty late on in the night. I don't remember just how late it was—half-past two, I think, or perhaps three—or, no, I don't remember. But, anyway, I was sitting up by myself very late reading. As I say, it was late, and, after all the noises in the street had stopped, the house somehow seemed to get awfully still and quiet. Well, all of a sudden I became aware of a sort of strange feeling—I hardly know how to describe it—I seemed to become aware of something, as if something were near me. I put down my book and looked around, but could see nothing. I started to read again, but I hadn't read more than a page, or say a page and a half—or no, not more than a page, when again all of a sudden I felt an overwhelming sense of—something. I can't explain just what the feeling was, but a queer sense as if there was something somewhere.

Well, I'm not of a timorous disposition naturally—at least I don't think I am—but absolutely I felt as if I couldn't stay in the room. I got up out of my chair and walked down the stairs, in the dark, to the dining-room. I felt all the way as if some one were following me. Do you know, I was absolutely trembling when I got into the dining-room and got the lights turned on. I walked over to the sideboard and poured myself out a drink of whisky and soda. As you know, I never take anything as a rule —or, at any rate, only when I am sitting round talking as we are now—but I always like to keep a decanter of whisky in the house, and a little soda, in case of my wife or one of the children being taken ill in the night.

Well, I took a drink and then I said to myself, I said, "See here, I'm going to see this thing through. " So I turned back and walked straight upstairs again to my room. I fully expected something queer was going to happen and was prepared for it. But do you know when I walked into the room again the feeling, or presentiment, or whatever it was I had had, was absolutely gone. There was my book lying just where I had left it and the reading lamp still burning on the table, just as it had been, and my chair just where I had pushed it back. But I felt nothing, absolutely nothing. I sat and waited awhile, but I still felt *nothing*.

I went downstairs again to put out the lights in the dining-room. I noticed as I passed the sideboard that I was still shaking a little. So I took a small drink of whisky—though as a rule I never care to take more than one drink—unless when I am sitting talking as we are here.

Well, I had hardly taken it when I felt an odd sort of psychic feeling—a sort of drowsiness. I remember, in a dim way, going to bed, and then I remember nothing till I woke up next morning.

And here's the strange part of it. I had hardly got down to the office after breakfast when I got a wire to tell me that my mother-in-law had broken her arm in Cincinnati. Strange, wasn't it? No, *not* at half-past two during that night—that's the inexplicable part of it. She had broken it at half-past eleven the morning before. But you notice it was *half-past* in each case. That's the queer way these things go.

Of course, I don't pretend to *explain it*. I suppose it simply means that I am telepathic—that's all. I imagine that, if I wanted to, I could talk with the dead and all that kind of thing. But I feel somehow that I don't want to.

Eh? Thank you, I will—though I seldom take more than— thanks, thanks, that's plenty of soda in it.

(III)

The familiar narrative in which the Successful Business Man recounts the early struggles by which he made good.

... No, sir, I had no early advantages whatever. I was brought up plain and hard—try one of these cigars; they cost me fifty cents each. In fact, I practically had no schooling at all. When I left school I didn't know how to read, not to read good. It's only since I've been in business that I've learned to write English, that is so as to use it right. But I'll guarantee to say there isn't a man in the shoe business to-day can write a better letter than I can. But all that I know is what I've learned myself. Why, I can't do fractions even now. I don't see that a man need. And I never learned no geography, except what I got for myself off railroad folders. I don't believe a man *needs* more than that anyway. I've got my boy at Harvard now. His mother was set on it. But I don't see that he learns anything, or nothing that will help him any in business. They say they learn them character and manners in the colleges, but, as I see it, a man can get all that just as well in business—is that wine all right? If not, tell me and I'll give the head waiter hell; they charge enough for it; what you're drinking costs me four-fifty a bottle.

But I was starting to tell you about my early start in business. I had it good and hard all right. Why when I struck New York—I was sixteen then—I had just eighty cents to my name. I lived on it for nearly a week while I was walking round hunting for a job. I used to get soup for three cents, and roast beef with potatoes, all you could eat, for eight cents, that tasted better than anything I can ever get in this damn club. It was down somewhere on Sixth Avenue, but I've forgotten the way to it.

Well, about the sixth day I got a job, down in a shoe factory, working on a machine. I guess you've never seen shoe-machinery, have you? No, you wouldn't likely. It's complicated. Even in those days there were thirty-five machines went to the making of a shoe, and now we use as many as fifty-four. I'd never seen the machines before, but the foreman took me on. "You look strong, " he said "I'll give you a try anyway. "

So I started in. I didn't know anything. But I made good from the first day. I got four a week at the start, and after two months I got a raise to four-twenty-five.

Well, after I'd worked there about three months, I went up to the floor manager of the flat I worked on, and I said, "Say, Mr. Jones, do you want to save ten dollars a week on expenses? " "How? " says he. "Why, " I said, "that foreman I'm working under on the machine, I've watched him, and I can do his job; dismiss him and I'll take over his work at half what you pay him. " "Can you do the work? " he says. "Try me out, " I said. "Fire him and give me a chance. " "Well," he said, "I like your spirit anyway; you've got the right sort of stuff in you. "

So he fired the foreman and I took over the job and held it down. It was hard at first, but I worked twelve hours a day, and studied up a book on factory machinery at night. Well, after I'd been on that work for about a year, I went in one day to the general manager downstairs, and I said, "Mr. Thompson, do you want to save about a hundred dollars a month on your overhead costs? " "How can I do that? " says he. "Sit down. " "Why, " I said, "you dismiss Mr. Jones and give me his place as manager of the floor, and I'll undertake to do his work, and mine with it, at a hundred less than you're paying now. " He turned and went into the inner office, and I could hear him talking to Mr. Evans, the managing director. "The young fellow certainly has character, " I heard him say. Then he came out and he said, "Well, we're going to give you a try anyway: we like to help out our employes all we can, you know; and you've got the sort of stuff in you that we're looking for. "

So they dismissed Jones next day and I took over his job and did it easy. It was nothing anyway. The higher up you get in business, the easier it is if you know how. I held that job two years, and I saved all my salary except twenty-five dollars a month, and I lived on that. I never spent any money anyway. I went once to see Irving do this Macbeth for twenty-five cents, and once I went to a concert and saw a man play the violin for fifteen cents in the gallery. But I don't believe you get much out of the theatre anyway; as I see it, there's nothing to it.

Well, after a while I went one day to Mr. Evans's office and I said, "Mr. Evans, I want you to dismiss Mr. Thompson, the general manager. " "Why, what's he done? " he says. "Nothing, " I said, "but I can take over his job on top of mine and you can pay me the salary you give him and save what you're paying me now. " "Sounds good to me, " he says.

So they let Thompson go and I took his place. That, of course, is where I got my real start, because, you see, I could control the output and run the costs up and down just where I liked. I suppose you don't know anything about costs and all that—they don't teach that sort of thing in colleges—but even you would understand something about dividends and would see that an energetic man with lots of character and business in him, If he's general manager can just do what he likes with the costs, especially the overhead, and the shareholders have just got to take what he gives them and be glad to. You see they can't fire him—not when he's got it all in his own hands—for fear it will all go to pieces.

Why would I want to run it that way for? Well, I'll tell you. I had a notion by that time that the business was getting so big that Mr. Evans, the managing director, and most of the board had pretty well lost track of the details and didn't understand it. There's an awful lot, you know, in the shoe business. It's not like ordinary things. It's complicated. And so I'd got an idea that I would shove them clean out of it—or most of them.

So I went one night to see the president, old Guggenbaum, up at his residence. He didn't only have this business, but he was in a lot of other things as well, and he was a mighty hard man to see. He wouldn't let any man see him unless he knew first what he was going to say. But I went up to his residence at night, and I saw him there. I talked first with his daughter, and I said I just had to see him. I said it so she didn't dare refuse. There's a way in talking to women that they won't say no.

So I showed Mr. Guggenbaum what I could do with the stock. "I can put that dividend, " I says, "clean down to zero—and they'll none of them know why. You can buy the lot of them out at your own price, and after that I'll put the dividend back to fifteen, or twenty, in two years. "

"And where do *you* come in? " says the old man, with a sort of hard look. He had a fine business head, the old man, at least in those days.

So I explained to him where I came in. "All right, " he said. "Go ahead. But I'll put nothing in writing. " "Mr. Guggenbaum, you don't need to, " I said. "You're as fair and square as I am and that's enough for me. "

His daughter let me out of the house door when I went. I guess she'd been pretty scared that she'd done wrong about letting me in. But I said to her it was all right, and after that when I wanted to see the old man I'd always ask for her and she'd see that I got in all right.

Got them squeezed out? Oh, yes, easy. There wasn't any trouble about that. You see the old man worked up a sort of jolt in wholesale leather on one side, and I fixed up a strike of the hands on the other. We passed the dividend two quarters running, and within a year we had them all scared out and the bulk of the little shareholders, of course, trooped out after them. They always do. The old man picked up the stock when they dropped it, and one-half of it he handed over to me.

That's what put me where I am now, do you see, with the whole control of the industry in two states and more than that now, because we have the Amalgamated Tanneries in with us, so it's practically all one concern.

Guggenbaum? Did I squeeze him out? No, I didn't because, you see, I didn't have to. The way it was—well, I tell you—I used to go up to the house, see, to arrange things with him—and the way it was— why, you see, I married his daughter, see, so I didn't exactly *need* to squeeze him out. He lives up with us now, but he's pretty old and past business. In fact, I do it all for him now, and pretty well everything he has is signed over to my wife. She has no head for it, and she's sort of timid anyway —always was—so I manage it all. Of course, if anything happens to the old man, then we get it all. I don't think he'll last long. I notice him each day, how weak he's getting.

My son in the business? Well, I'd like him to be. But he don't seem to take to it somehow—I'm afraid he takes more after his mother; or else it's the college that's doing it. Somehow, I don't think the colleges bring out business character, do you?

X. A Study in Still Life—My Tailor

He always stands there—and has stood these thirty years—in the back part of his shop, his tape woven about his neck, a smile of welcome on his face, waiting to greet me.

"Something in a serge, " he says, "or perhaps in a tweed? "

There are only these two choices open to us. We have had no others for thirty years. It is too late to alter now.

"A serge, yes, " continues my tailor, "something in a dark blue, perhaps. " He says it with all the gusto of a new idea, as if the thought of dark blue had sprung up as an inspiration. "Mr. Jennings" (this is his assistant), "kindly take down some of those dark blues.

"Ah, " he exclaims, "now here is an excellent thing. " His manner as he says this is such as to suggest that by sheer good fortune and blind chance he has stumbled upon a thing among a million.

He lifts one knee and drapes the cloth over it, standing upon one leg. He knows that in this attitude it is hard to resist him. Cloth to be appreciated as cloth must be viewed over the bended knee of a tailor with one leg in the air.

My tailor can stand in this way indefinitely, on one leg in a sort of ecstasy, a kind of local paralysis.

"Would that make up well? " I ask him.

"Admirably, " he answers.

I have no real reason to doubt it. I have never seen any reason why cloth should not make up well. But I always ask the question as I know that he expects it and it pleases him. There ought to be a fair give and take in such things.

"You don't think it at all loud? " I say. He always likes to be asked this.

"Oh, no, very quiet indeed. In fact we always recommend serge as extremely quiet. "

I have never had a wild suit in my life. But it is well to ask.

Then he measures me—round the chest, nowhere else. All the other measures were taken years ago. Even the chest measure is only done—and I know it—to please me. I do not really grow.

"A *little* fuller in the chest, " my tailor muses. Then he turns to his assistant. "Mr. Jennings, a little fuller in the chest—half an inch on to the chest, please. "

It is a kind fiction. Growth around the chest is flattering even to the humblest of us.

"Yes, " my tailor goes on—he uses "yes" without any special meaning—"and shall we say a week from Tuesday? Mr. Jennings, a week from Tuesday, please. "

"And will you please, " I say, "send the bill to—? " but my tailor waves this aside. He does not care to talk about the bill. It would only give pain to both of us to speak of it.

The bill is a matter we deal with solely by correspondence, and that only in a decorous and refined style never calculated to hurt.

I am sure from the tone of my tailor's letters that he would never send the bill, or ask for the amount, were it not that from time to time he is himself, unfortunately, "pressed" owing to "large consignments from Europe. " But for these heavy consignments, I am sure I should never need to pay him. It is true that I have sometimes thought to observe that these consignments are apt to arrive when I pass the limit of owing for two suits and order a third. But this can only be a mere coincidence.

Yet the bill, as I say, is a thing that we never speak of. Instead of it my tailor passes to the weather. Ordinary people always begin with this topic. Tailors, I notice, end with it. It is only broached after the suit is ordered, never before.

"Pleasant weather we are having, " he says. It is never other, so I notice, with him. Perhaps the order of a suit itself is a little beam of sunshine.

Then we move together towards the front of the store on the way to the outer door.

"Nothing to-day, I suppose, " says my tailor, "in shirtings? "

"No, thank you. "

This is again a mere form. In thirty years I have never bought any shirtings from him. Yet he asks the question with the same winsomeness as he did thirty years ago.

"And nothing, I suppose, in collaring or in hosiery? "

This is again futile. Collars I buy elsewhere and hosiery I have never worn.

Thus we walk to the door, in friendly colloquy. Somehow if he failed to speak of shirtings and hosiery, I should feel as if a familiar cord had broken;

At the door we part.

"Good afternoon, " he says. "A week from Tuesday—yes —good afternoon. "

Such is—or was—our calm unsullied intercourse, unvaried or at least broken only by consignments from Europe.

I say it *was*, that is until just the other day.

And then, coming to the familiar door, for my customary summer suit, I found that he was there no more. There were people in the store, unloading shelves and piling cloth and taking stock. And they told me that he was dead. It came to me with a strange shock. I had not thought it possible. He seemed—he should have been — immortal.

They said the worry of his business had helped to kill him. I could not have believed it. It always seemed so still and tranquil—weaving his tape about his neck and marking measures and holding cloth against his leg beside the sunlight of the window in the back part of the shop. Can a man die of that? Yet he had been "going behind, " they said (however that is done), for years. His wife, they told me, would be left badly off. I had never conceived him as having a wife. But it seemed that he had, and a daughter, too, at a conservatory of music —yet he never spoke of her—and that he himself was musical and played the flute, and was the sidesman of a church—yet he never referred to it to me. In fact, in thirty years we never spoke of religion. It was hard to connect him with the idea of it.

As I went out I seemed to hear his voice still saying, "And nothing to-day in shirtings? "

I was sorry I had never bought any.

There is, I am certain, a deep moral in this. But I will not try to draw it. It might appear too obvious.

Peace, War, and Politics

XI. Germany from Within Out

The adventure which I here narrate resulted out of a strange psychological experience of a kind that (outside of Germany) would pass the bounds of comprehension.

To begin with, I had fallen asleep.

Of the reason for my falling asleep I have no doubt. I had remained awake nearly the whole of the preceding night, absorbed in the perusal of a number of recent magazine articles and books dealing with Germany as seen from within. I had read from cover to cover that charming book, just written by Lady de Washaway, under the title *Ten Years as a Toady, or The Per-Hapsburgs as I Didn't Know Them*. Her account of the life of the Imperial Family of Austria, simple, unaffected, home-like; her picture of the good old Emperor, dining quietly off a cold potato and sitting after dinner playing softly to himself on the flute, while his attendants gently withdrew one by one from his presence; her description of merry, boisterous, large-hearted Prince Stefan Karl, who kept the whole court in a perpetual roar all the time by asking such riddles as "When is a sailor not a sailor? " (the answer being, of course, when he is a German Prince) — in fact, the whole book had thrilled me to the verge of spiritual exhaustion.

From Lady de Washaway's work I turned to peruse Hugo von Halbwitz's admirable book, *Easy Marks, or How the German Government Borrows its Funds*; and after that I had read Karl von Wiggleround's *Despatches* and Barnstuff's *Confidential Letters to Criminals*.

As a consequence I fell asleep as if poisoned.

But the amazing thing is that, whenever it was or was not that I fell asleep, I woke up to find myself in Germany.

I cannot offer any explanation as to how this came about. I merely state the fact.

There I was, seated on the grassy bank of a country road.

I knew it was Germany at once. There was no mistaking it. The whole landscape had an orderliness, a method about it that is, alas, never seen in British countries. The trees stood in neat lines, with the name of each nailed to it on a board. The birds sat in regular rows, four to a branch, and sang in harmony, very simply, but with the true German feeling.

There were two peasants working beside the road. One was picking up fallen leaves, and putting them into neat packets of fifty. The other was cutting off the tops of the late thistles that still stood unwithered in the chill winter air, and arranging them according to size and colour. In Germany nothing is lost; nothing is wasted. It is perhaps not generally known that from the top of the thistle the Germans obtain picrate of ammonia, the most deadly explosive known to modern chemistry, while from the bulb below, butter, crude rubber and sweet cider are extracted in large quantities.

The two peasants paused in their work a moment as they saw me glance towards them, and each, with the simple gentility of the German working man, quietly stood on his head until I had finished looking at him.

I felt quite certain, of course, that it must only be a matter of a short time before I would inevitably be arrested.

I felt doubly certain of it when I saw a motor speeding towards me with a stout man, in military uniform and a Prussian helmet, seated behind the chauffeur.

The motor stopped, but to my surprise the military man, whom I perceived to be wearing the uniform of a general, jumped out and advanced towards me with a genial cry of:

"Well, Herr Professor! "

I looked at him again.

"Why, Fritz! " I cried.

"You recognize me? " he said.

"Certainly, " I answered, "you used to be one of the six German waiters at McCluskey's restaurant in Toronto. "

Further Foolishness

The General laughed.

"You really took us for waiters! " he said. "Well, well. My dear professor! How odd! We were all generals in the German army. My own name is not Fritz Schmidt, as you knew it, but Count von Boobenstein. The Boobs of Boobenstein, " he added proudly, "are connected with the Hohenzollerns. When I am commanded to dine with the Emperor, I have the hereditary right to eat anything that he leaves. "

"But I don't understand! " I said. "Why were you in Toronto? "

"Perfectly simple. Special military service. We were there to make a report. Each day we kept a record of the velocity and direction of the wind, the humidity of the air, the distance across King Street and the height of the C. P.R. Building. All this we wired to Germany every day. "

"For what purpose? " I asked.

"Pardon me! " said the General, and then, turning the subject with exquisite tact: "Do you remember Max? " he said.

"Do you mean the tall melancholy looking waiter, who used to eat the spare oysters and drink up what was left in the glasses, behind the screen? "

"Ha! " exclaimed my friend. "But *why* did he drink them? *Why?* Do you know that that man—his real name is not Max but Ernst Niedelfein—is one of the greatest chemists in Germany? Do you realise that he was making a report to our War Office on the percentage of alcohol obtainable in Toronto after closing time? "

"And Karl? " I asked.

"Karl was a topographist in the service of his High Serenity the King Regnant of Bavaria"—here my friend saluted himself with both hands and blinked his eyes four times—"He made maps of all the breweries of Canada. We know now to a bottle how many German soldiers could be used in invading Canada without danger of death from drought. "

"How many was it? " I asked.

Boobenstein shook his head.

"Very disappointing, " he said. "In fact your country is not yet ripe for German occupation. Our experts say that the invasion of Canada is an impossibility unless we use Milwaukee as a base—But step into my motor, " said the Count, interrupting himself, "and come along with me. Stop, you are cold. This morning air is very keen. Take this, " he added, picking off the fur cap from the chauffeur's head. "It will be better than that hat you are wearing—or, here, wait a moment—"

As he spoke, the Count unwound a woollen muffler from the chauffeur's neck, and placed it round mine.

"Now then, " he added, "this sheepskin coat—"

"My dear Count, " I protested.

"Not a bit, not a bit, " he cried, as he pulled off the chauffeur's coat and shoved me into it. His face beamed with true German generosity.

"Now, " he said as we settled back into the motor and started along the road, "I am entirely at your service. Try one of these cigars! Got it alight? Right! You notice, no doubt, the exquisite flavour. It is a *Tannhauser.* Our chemists are making these cigars now out of the refuse of the tanneries and glue factories. "

I sighed involuntarily. Imagine trying to "blockade" a people who could make cigars out of refuse; imagine trying to get near them at all!

"Strong, aren't they? " said von Boobenstein, blowing a big puff of smoke. "In fact, it is these cigars that have given rise to the legend (a pure fiction, I need hardly say) that our armies are using asphyxiating gas. The truth is they are merely smoking German-made tobacco in their trenches. "

"But come now, " he continued, "your meeting me is most fortunate. Let me explain. I am at present on the Intelligence Branch of the General Staff. My particular employment is dealing with foreign visitors—the branch of our service called, for short, the Eingewanderte Fremden Verfullungs Bureau. How would you call that? "

"It sounds, " I said, "like the Bureau for Stuffing Up Incidental Foreigners. "

"Precisely, " said the Count, "though your language lacks the music of ours. It is my business to escort visitors round Germany and help them with their despatches. I took the Ford party through—in a closed cattle-car, with the lights out. They were greatly impressed. They said that, though they saw nothing, they got an excellent idea of the atmosphere of Germany. It was I who introduced Lady de Washaway to the Court of Franz Joseph. I write the despatches from Karl von Wiggleround, and send the necessary material to Ambassador von Barnstuff. In fact I can take you everywhere, show you everything, and" —here my companion's military manner suddenly seemed to change into something obsequiously and strangely familiar—"it won't cost you a cent; not a cent, unless you care—"

I understood.

I handed him ten cents.

"Thank you, sir, " he said. Then with an abrupt change back to his military manner, "Now, then, what would you like to see? The army? The breweries? The Royal court? Berlin? What shall it be? My time is limited, but I shall be delighted to put myself at your service for the rest of the day. "

"I think, " I said, "I should like more than anything to see Berlin, if it is possible. "

"Possible? " answered my companion. "Nothing easier. "

The motor flew ahead and in a few moments later we were making our arrangements with a local station-master for a special train to Berlin.

I got here my first glimpse of the wonderful perfection of the German railway system.

"I am afraid, " said the station-master, with deep apologies, "that I must ask you to wait half an hour. I am moving a quarter of a million troops from the east to the west front, and this always holds up the traffic for fifteen or twenty minutes. "

I stood on the platform watching the troops trains go by and admiring the marvellous ingenuity of the German system.

As each train went past at full speed, a postal train (Feld-Post-Eisenbahn-Zug) moved on the other track in the opposite direction, from which a shower of letters were thrown in to the soldiers through the window. Immediately after the postal train, a soup train (Soup-Zug) was drawn along, from the windows of which soup was squirted out of a hose.

Following this there came at full speed a beer train (Bier-Zug) from which beer bombs were exploded in all directions.

I watched till all had passed.

"Now, " said the station-master, "your train is ready. Here you are. "

Away we sped through the meadows and fields, hills and valleys, forests and plains.

And nowhere—I am forced, like all other travellers, to admit it—did we see any signs of the existence of war. Everything was quiet, orderly, usual. We saw peasants digging—in an orderly way—for acorns in the frozen ground. We saw little groups of soldiers drilling in the open squares of villages—in their quiet German fashion — each man chained by the leg to the man next to him; here and there great Zeppelins sailed overhead dropping bombs, for practice, on the less important towns; at times in the village squares we saw clusters of haggard women (quite quiet and orderly) waving little red flags and calling: "Bread, bread! "

But nowhere any signs of war. Certainly not.

We reached Berlin just at nightfall. I had expected to find it changed. To my surprise it appeared just as usual. The streets were brilliantly lighted. Music burst in waves from the restaurants. From the theatre signs I saw, to my surprise, that they were playing *Hamlet*, *East Lynne* and *Potash and Perlmutter*. Everywhere was brightness, gaiety and light-heartedness.

Here and there a merry-looking fellow, with a brush and a pail of paste and a roll of papers over his arm, would swab up a casualty list of two or three thousand names, amid roars of good-natured laughter.

What perplexed me most was the sight of thousands of men, not in uniform, but in ordinary civilian dress.

"Boobenstein, " I said, as we walked down the Linden Avenue, "I don't understand it. "

"The men? " he answered. "It's a perfectly simple matter. I see you don't understand our army statistics. At the beginning of the war we had an army of three million. Very good. Of these, one million were in the reserve. We called them to the colours, that made four million. Then of these all who wished were allowed to volunteer for special services. Half a million did so. That made four and a half million. In the first year of the war we suffered two million casualties, but of these seventy-five per cent, or one and a half million, returned later on to the colours, bringing our grand total up to six million. This six million we use on each of six fronts, giving a grand total of thirty six million.

"I see, " I said. "In fact, I have seen these figures before. In other words, your men are inexhaustible. "

"Precisely, " said the Count, "and mark you, behind these we still have the Landsturm, made up of men between fifty-five and sixty, and the Landslide, reputed to be the most terrible of all the German levies, made up by withdrawing the men from the breweries. That is the last final act of national fury. But come, " he said, "you must be hungry. Is it not so? "

"I am, " I admitted, "but I had hesitated to acknowledge it. I feared that the food supply—"

Boobenstein broke into hearty laughter.

"Food supply! " he roared. "My dear fellow, you must have been reading the English newspapers! Food supply! My dear professor! Have you not heard? We have got over that difficulty entirely and for ever. But come, here is a restaurant. In with you and eat to your heart's content. "

We entered the restaurant. It was filled to overflowing with a laughing crowd of diners and merry-makers. Thick clouds of blue cigar smoke filled the air. Waiters ran to and fro with tall steins of foaming beer, and great bundles of bread tickets, soup tickets, meat cards and butter coupons.

These were handed around to the guests, who sat quietly chewing the corners of them as they sipped their beer.

"Now-then, " said my host, looking over the printed menu in front of him, "what shall it be? What do you say to a ham certificate with a cabbage ticket on the side? Or how would you like lobster-coupon with a receipt for asparagus? "

"Yes, " I answered, "or perhaps, as our journey has made me hungry, one of these beef certificates with an affidavit for Yorkshire pudding. "

"Done! " said Boobenstein.

A few moments later we were comfortably drinking our tall glasses of beer and smoking *Tannhauser* cigars, with an appetising pile of coloured tickets and certificates in front of us.

"Admit, " said von Boobenstein good-naturedly, "that we have overcome the food difficulty for ever. "

"You have, " I said.

"It was a pure matter of science and efficiency, " he went on. "It has long been observed that if one sat down in a restaurant and drank beer and smoked cigars (especially such a brand as these *Tannhausers*) during the time it took for the food to be brought (by a German waiter), all appetite was gone. It remained for the German scientists to organise this into system. Have you finished? Or would you like to take another look at your beef certificate? "

We rose. Von Boobenstein paid the bill by writing I. O.U. on the back of one of the cards—not forgetting the waiter, for whom he wrote on a piece of paper, "God bless you"—and we left.

"Count, " I said, as we took our seat on a bench in the Sieges-Allee, or Alley of Victory, and listened to the music of the military band,

and watched the crowd, "I begin to see that Germany is unconquerable. "

"Absolutely so, " he answered.

"In the first place, your men are inexhaustible. If we kill one class you call out another; and anyway one-half of those we kill get well again, and the net result is that you have more than ever. "

"Precisely, " said the Count.

"As to food, " I continued, "you are absolutely invulnerable. What with acorns, thistles, tanbark, glue, tickets, coupons, and certificates, you can go on for ever. "

"We can, " he said.

"Then for money you use I. O.U. 's. Anybody with a lead pencil can command all the funds he wants. Moreover, your soldiers at the front are getting dug in deeper and deeper: last spring they were fifty feet under ground: by 1918 they will be nearly 200 feet down. Short of mining for them, we shall never get them out. "

"Never, " said von Boobenstein with great firmness.

"But there is one thing that I don't quite understand. Your navy, your ships. There, surely, we have you: sooner or later that whole proud fleet in the Kiel Canal will come out under fire of our guns and be sunk to the bottom of the sea. There, at least, we conquer. "

Von Boobenstein broke into loud laughter.

"The fleet! " he roared, and his voice was almost hysterical and overstrung, as if high living on lobster-coupons and over-smoking of *Tannhausers* was undermining his nerves. "The fleet! Is it possible you do not know? Why all Germany knows it. Capture our fleet! Ha! Ha! It now lies fifty miles inland. *We have filled in the canal*—pushed in the banks. The canal is solid land again, and the fleet is high and dry. The ships are boarded over and painted to look like German inns and breweries. Prinz Adelbert is disguised as a brewer, Admiral von Tirpitz is made up as a head waiter, Prince Heinrich is a bar tender, the sailors are dressed up as chambermaids. And some day when Jellicoe and his men are coaxed ashore, they will drop in to drink a glass of beer, and then—pouf! we will explode them all with a single torpedo! Such is the naval strategy of our scientists! Are we not a nation of sailors? "

Von Boobenstein's manner had grown still wilder and more hysterical. There was a queer glitter in his eyes.

I thought it better to soothe him.

"I see, " I said, "the Allies are beaten. One might as well spin a coin for heads or tails to see whether we abandon England now or wait till you come and take it. "

As I spoke, I took from my pocket an English sovereign that I carry as a lucky-piece, and prepared to spin it in the air.

Von Boobenstein, as he saw it, broke into a sort of hoarse shriek.

"Gold! gold! " he cried. "Give it to me! "

"What? " I exclaimed.

"A piece of gold, " he panted. "Give it to me, give it to me, quick. I know a place where we can buy bread with it. Real bread—not tickets—food—give me the gold—gold—for bread—we can get bread. I am starving—gold—bread. "

And as he spoke his hoarse voice seemed to grow louder and louder in my ears; the sounds of the street were hushed; a sudden darkness fell; and a wind swept among the trees of the *Alley of Victory*—moaning—and a thousand, a myriad voices seemed to my ear to take up the cry:

"Gold! Bread! We are starving. "

Then I woke up.

XII. Abdul Aziz has His:
An Adventure in the Yildiz Kiosk

"Come, come, Abdul, " I said, putting my hand, not unkindly, on his shoulder, "tell me all about it. "

But he only broke out into renewed sobbing.

"There, there, " I continued soothingly. "Don't cry, Abdul. Look! Here's a lovely narghileh for you to smoke, with a gold mouthpiece. See! Wouldn't you like a little latakia, eh? And here's a little toy Armenian—look! See his head come off—snick! There, it's on again, snick! now it's off! look, Abdul! "

But still he sobbed.

His fez had fallen over his ears and his face was all smudged with tears.

It seemed impossible to stop him.

I looked about in vain from the little alcove of the hall of the Yildiz Kiosk where we were sitting on a Persian bench under a lemon-tree. There was no one in sight. I hardly knew what to do.

In the Yildiz Kiosk—I think that was the name of the place—I scarcely as yet knew my way about. In fact, I had only been in it a few hours. I had come there—as I should have explained in commencing—in order to try to pick up information as to the exact condition of things in Turkey. For this purpose I had assumed the character and disguise of an English governess. I had long since remarked that an English governess is able to go anywhere, see everything, penetrate the interior of any royal palace and move to and fro as she pleases without hindrance and without insult. No barrier can stop her. Every royal court, however splendid or however exclusive, is glad to get her. She dines with the King or the Emperor as a matter of course. All state secrets are freely confided to her and all military plans are submitted to her judgment. Then, after a few weeks' residence, she leaves the court and writes a book of disclosures.

This was now my plan.

And, up to the moment of which I speak, it had worked perfectly.

I had found my way through Turkey to the royal capital without difficulty. The poke bonnet, the spectacles and the long black dress which I had assumed had proved an ample protection. None of the rude Turkish soldiers among whom I had passed had offered to lay a hand on me. This tribute I am compelled to pay to the splendid morality of the Turks. They wouldn't touch me.

Access to the Yildiz Kiosk and to the Sultan had proved equally easy. I had merely to obtain an interview with Codfish Pasha, the Secretary of War, whom I found a charming man of great intelligence, a master of three or four languages (as he himself informed me), and able to count up to seventeen.

"You wish, " he said, "to be appointed as English, or rather Canadian governess to the Sultan? "

"Yes, " I answered.

"And your object? "

"I propose to write a book of disclosures. "

"Excellent, " said Codfish.

An hour later I found myself, as I have said, in a flag-stoned hall of the Yildiz Kiosk, with the task of amusing and entertaining the Sultan.

Of the difficulty of this task I had formed no conception. Here I was at the outset, with the unhappy Abdul bent and broken with sobs which I found no power to check or control.

Naturally, therefore, I found myself at a loss. The little man as he sat on his cushions, in his queer costume and his long slippers with his fez fallen over his lemon-coloured face, presented such a pathetic object that I could not find the heart to be stern with him.

"Come, now, Abdul, " I said, "be good! "

He paused a moment in his crying—

"Why do you call me Abdul? " he asked. "That isn't my name. "

"Isn't it? " I said. "I thought all you Sultans were called Abdul. Isn't the Sultan's name always Abdul? "

"Mine isn't, " he whimpered, "but it doesn't matter, " and his face began to crinkle up with renewed weeping. "Call me anything you like. It doesn't matter. Anyway I'd rather be called Abdul than be called a W-W-War Lord and a G-G-General when they won't let me have any say at all—"

And with that the little Sultan burst into unrestrained crying.

"Abdul, " I said firmly, "if you don't stop crying, I'll go and fetch one of the Bashi-Bazouks to take you away. "

The little Sultan found his voice again.

"There aren't any Bub-Bub-Bashi-Bazouks left, " he sobbed.

"None left? " I exclaimed. "Where are they gone? "

"They've t-t-taken them all aw-w-way—"

"Who have? "

"The G-G-G-Germans, " sobbed Abdul. "And they've sent them all to P-P-P-Poland. "

"Come, come, Abdul, " I said, straightening him up a little as he sat. "Brace up! Be a Turk! Be a Mohammedan! Don't act like a Christian."

This seemed to touch his pride. He made a great effort to be calm. I could hear him muttering to himself, "Allah, Illallah, Mohammed rasoul Allah! " He said this over a good many times, while I took advantage of the pause to get his fez a little straighter and wipe his face.

"How many times have I said it? " he asked presently.

"Twenty. "

"Twenty? That ought to be enough, shouldn't it? " said the Sultan, regaining himself a little. "Isn't prayer helpful, eh? Give me a smoke?"

I filled his narghileh for him, and he began to suck blue smoke out of it with a certain contentment, while the rose water bubbled in the bowl below.

"Now, Abdul, " I said, as I straightened up his cushions and made him a little more comfortable, "what is it? What is the matter? "

"Why, " he answered, "they've all g-g-gone—"

"Now, don't cry! Tell me properly. "

"They've all gone b-b-back on me! Boo-hoo! "

"Who have? Who've gone back on you? "

"Why, everybody. The English and the French and everybody—"

"What *do* you mean? " I asked with increasing interest. "Tell me exactly what you mean. Whatever you say I will hold sacred, of course. "

I saw my part already to a volume of interesting disclosures.

"They used to treat me so differently, " Abdul went on, and his sobbing ceased as he continued, "They used to call me the Bully Boy of the Bosphorus. They said I was the Guardian of the Golden Gate. They used to let me kill all the Armenians I liked and nobody was allowed to collect debts from me, and every now and then they used to send me the nicest ultimatums—Oh, you don't know, " he broke off, "how nice it used to be here in the Yildiz in the old days! We used all to sit round here, in this very hall, me and the diplomats, and play games, such as 'Ultimatum, ultimatum, who's got the ultimatum. ' Oh, say, it was so nice and peaceful! And we used to have big dinners and conferences, especially after the military manoeuvres and the autumn massacres—me and the diplomats, all with stars and orders, and me in my white fez with a copper tassel— and hold discussions about how to reform Macedonia. "

"But you spoilt it all, Abdul, " I protested.

"I didn't, I didn't! " he exclaimed almost angrily. "I'd have gone on for ever. It was all so nice. They used to present me—the diplomats did—with what they called their Minimum, and then we (I mean Codfish Pasha and me) had to draft in return our Maximum—see? — and then we all had to get together again and frame a *status quo.* "

"But that couldn't go on for ever, " I urged.

"Why not? " said Abdul. "It was a great system. We invented it, but everybody was beginning to copy it. In fact, we were leading the world, before all this trouble came. Didn't you have anything of our system in your country —what do you call it—in Canada? "

"Yes, " I admitted. "Now that I come to think of it, we were getting into it. But the war has changed it all—"

"Exactly, " said Abdul. "There you are! All changed! The good old days gone for ever! "

"But surely, " I said, "you still have friends—the Bulgarians. "

The Sultan's little black eyes flashed with anger as he withdrew his pipe for a moment from his mouth.

"The low scoundrels! " he said between his teeth. "The traitors! "

"Why, they're your Allies! "

"Yes, Allah destroy them! They are. They've come over to *our* side. After centuries of fighting they refuse to play fair any longer. They're on *our* side! Who ever heard of such a thing? Bah! But, of course, " he added more quietly, "we shall massacre them just the same. We shall insist, in the terms of peace, on retaining our rights of massacre. But then, no doubt, all the nations will. "

"But you have the Germans—" I began.

"Hush, hush, " said Abdul, laying his hand on my arm. "Some one might hear. "

"You have the Germans, " I repeated.

"The Germans, " said Abdul, and his voice sounded in a queer sing-song like that of a child repeating a lesson, "are my noble friends, the Germans are my powerful allies, the Kaiser is my good brother, the Reichstag is my foster-sister. I love the Germans. I hate the English. I love the Kaiser. The Kaiser loves me—"

"Stop, stop, Abdul, " I said, "who taught you all that? "

Abdul looked cautiously around.

"*They* did, " he said in a whisper. "There's a lot more of it. Would you like me to recite some more? Or, no, no, what's the good? I've no heart for reciting any longer. " And at this Abdul fell to weeping again.

"But, Abdul, " I said, "I don't understand. Why are you so distressed just now? All this has been going on for over two years. Why are you so worried just now? "

"Oh, " exclaimed the little Sultan in surprise, "you haven't heard! I see—you've only just arrived. Why, to-day is the last day. After to-day it is all over. "

"Last day for what? " I asked.

"For intervention. For the intervention of the United States. The only thing that can save us. It was to have come to-day, by the end of this full moon—our astrologers had predicted it—Smith Pasha, Minister under Heaven of the United States, had promised, if it came, to send it to us at the earliest moment. How do they send it, do you know, in a box, or in paper? "

"Stop, " I said as my ear caught the sound of footsteps. "There's some one coming now. "

The sound of slippered feet was distinctly heard on the stones in the outer corridor.

Abdul listened intently a moment.

"I know his slippers, " he said.

"Who is it? "

"It is my chief secretary, Toomuch Koffi. Yes, here he comes. "

As the Sultan spoke, the doors swung open and there entered an aged Turk, in a flowing gown and coloured turban, with a melancholy yellow face, and a long white beard that swept to his girdle.

"Who do you say he is? " I whispered to Abdul.

"My chief secretary, " he whispered back. "Toomuch Koffi. "

"He looks like it, " I murmured.

Meantime, Toomuch Koffi had advanced across the broad flagstones of the hall where we were sitting. With hands lifted he salaamed four times—east, west, north, and south.

"What does that mean? " I whispered.

"It means, " said the Sultan, with visible agitation, "that he has a communication of the greatest importance and urgency, which will not brook a moment's delay. "

"Well, then, why doesn't he get a move on? " I whispered.

"Hush, " said Abdul.

Toomuch Koffi now straightened himself from his last salaam and spoke.

"Allah is great! " he said.

"And Mohammed is his prophet, " rejoined the Sultan.

"Allah protect you! And make your face shine, " said Toomuch.

"Allah lengthen your beard, " said the Sultan, and he added aside to me in English, which Toomuch Koffi evidently did not understand, "I'm all eagerness to know what it is—it's something big, for sure. " The little man was quite quivering with excitement as he spoke. "Do you know what I think it is? I think it must be the American Intervention. The United States is going to intervene. Eh? What? Don't you think so? "

"Then hurry him up, " I urged.

"I can't, " said Abdul. "It is impossible in Turkey to do business like that. He must have some coffee first and then he must pray and then there must be an interchange of presents. "

I groaned, for I was getting as impatient as Abdul himself.

"Do you not do public business like that in Canada? " the Sultan continued.

"We used to. But we have got over it, " I said.

Meanwhile a slippered attendant had entered and placed a cushion for the secretary, and in front of it a little Persian stool on which he put a quaint cup filled with coffee black as ink.

A similar cup was placed before the Sultan.

"Drink! " said Abdul.

"Not first, until the lips of the Commander of the Faithful—"

"He means 'after you, '" I said. "Hurry up, Abdul. "

Abdul took a sip.

"Allah is good, " he said.

"And all things are of Allah, " rejoined Toomuch.

Abdul unpinned a glittering jewel from his robe and threw it to the feet of Toomuch.

"Take this poor bauble, " he said.

Toomuch Koffi in return took from his wrist a solid bangle of beaten gold.

"Accept this mean gift from your humble servant, " he said.

"Right! " said Abdul, speaking in a changed voice as the ceremonies ended. "Now, then, Toomuch, what is it? Hurry up. Be quick. What is the matter? "

Toomuch rose to his feet, lifted his hands high in the air with the palms facing the Sultan.

"One is without, " he said.

"Without what? " I asked eagerly of the Sultan.

"Without—outside. Don't you understand Turkish? What you call in English—a gentleman to see me. "

"And did he make all that fuss and delay over that? " I asked in disgust. "Why with us in Canada, at one of the public departments of Ottawa, all that one would have to do would be simply to send in a card, get it certified, then simply wait in an anteroom, simply read a newspaper, send in another card, wait a little, then simply send in a third card, and then simply—"

"Pshaw! " said Abdul. "The cards might be poisoned. Our system is best. Speak on, Toomuch. Who is without? Is it perchance a messenger from Smith Pasha, Minister under Heaven of the United States? "

"Alas, no! " said Toomuch. "It is HE. It is THE LARGE ONE! "

As he spoke he rolled his eyes upward with a gesture of despair.

"HE! " cried Abdul, and a look of terror convulsed his face. "The Large One! Shut him out! Call the Chief Eunuch and the Major Domo of the Harem! Let him not in! "

"Alas, " said Toomuch, "he threw them out of the window. Lo! he is here, he enters. "

As the secretary spoke, a double door at the end of the hall swung noisily open, at the blow of an imperious fist, and with a rattle of arms and accoutrements a man of gigantic stature, wearing full military uniform and a spiked helmet, strode into the room.

As he entered, an attendant who accompanied him, also in a uniform and a spiked helmet, called in a loud strident voice that resounded to the arches of the hall:

"His High Excellenz Feld Marechal von der Doppelbauch, Spezial Representant of His Majestat William II, Deutscher Kaiser and King of England! "

Abdul collapsed into a little heap. His fez fell over his face. Toomuch Koffi had slunk into a corner.

Von der Doppelbauch strode noisily forward and came to a stand in front of Abdul with a click and rattle after the Prussian fashion.

"Majestat, " he said in a deep, thunderous voice, "I greet you. I bow low before you. Salaam! I kiss the floor at your feet. "

But in reality he did nothing of the sort. He stood to the full height of his six feet six and glowered about him.

"Salaam! " said Abdul, in a feeble voice.

"But who is this? " added the Field-Marshal, looking angrily at me.

My costume, or rather my disguise, for, as I have said, I was wearing a poke bonnet with a plain black dress, seemed to puzzle him.

"My new governess, " said Abdul. "She came this morning. She is a professor—"

"Bah! " said the Field-Marshal, "a *woman* a professor! Bah! "

"No, no, " said Abdul in protest, and it seemed decent of the little creature to stick up for me. "She's all right, she is interesting and knows a great deal. She's from Canada! "

"What! " exclaimed Von der Doppelbauch. "From Canada! But stop! It seems to me that Canada is a country that we are at war with. Let me think, Canada? I must look at my list"—he pulled out a little set of tablets as he spoke—"let me see, Britain, Great Britain, British North America, British Guiana, British Nigeria—ha! of course, under K—Kandahar, Korfu. No, I don't seem to see it—Fritz, " he called to the aide-de-camp who had announced him, "telegraph at once to the

Topographical Staff at Berlin and find out if we are at war with Canada. If we are"—he pointed at me—"throw her into the Bosphorus. If we are not, treat her with every consideration, with every distinguished consideration. But see that she doesn't get away. Keep her tight, till we *are* at war with Canada, as no doubt we shall be, wherever it is, and *then* throw her into the Bosphorus. "

The aide clicked his heels and withdrew.

"And now, your majesty, " continued the Field-Marshal, turning abruptly to the Sultan, "I bring you good news. "

"More good news, " groaned Abdul miserably, winding his clasped fingers to and fro. "Alas, good news again! "

"First, " said Von der Doppelbauch, "the Kaiser has raised you to the order of the Black Dock. Here is your feather. "

"Another feather, " moaned Abdul. "Here, Toomuch, take it and put it among the feathers! "

"Secondly, " went on the Field-Marshal, checking off his items as he spoke, "your contribution, your personal contribution to His Majesty's Twenty-third Imperial Loan, is accepted. "

"I didn't make any! " sobbed Abdul.

"No difference, " said Von der Doppelbauch. "It is accepted anyway. The telegram has just arrived accepting all your money. My assistants are packing it up outside. "

Abdul collapsed still further into his cushions.

"Third, and this will rejoice your Majesty's heart: Your troops are again victorious! "

"Victorious! " moaned Abdul. "Victorious again! I knew they would be! I suppose they are all dead as usual? "

"They are, " said the Marshal. "Their souls, " he added reverently, with a military salute, "are in Heaven! "

"No, no, " gasped Abdul, "not in Heaven! don't say that! Not in Heaven! Say that they are in Nishvana, our Turkish paradise. "

"I am sorry, " said the Field-Marshal gravely. "This is a Christian war. The Kaiser has insisted on their going to Heaven. "

The Sultan bowed his head.

"Ishmillah! " he murmured. "It is the will of Allah. "

"But they did not die without glory, " went on the Field-Marshal. "Their victory was complete. Set it out to yourself, " and here his eyes glittered with soldierly passion. "There stood your troops—ten thousand! In front of them the Russians—a hundred thousand. What did your men do? Did they pause? No, they charged! "

"They *charged!* " cried the Sultan in misery. "Don't say that! Have they charged again! Just Allah! " he added, turning to Toomuch. "They have charged again! And we must pay, we shall have to pay— we always do when they charge. Alas, alas, they have charged again. Everything is charged! "

"But how nobly, " rejoined the Prussian. "Imagine it to yourself! Here, beside this stool, let us say, were your men. There, across the cushion, were the Russians. All the ground between was mined. We knew it. Our soldiers knew it. Even our staff knew it. Even Prinz Tattelwitz Halfstuff, our commander, knew it. But your soldiers did not. What did our Prinz do? The Prinz called for volunteers to charge over the ground. There was a great shout—from our men, our German regiments. He called again. There was another shout. He called still again. There was a third shout. Think of it! And again Prinz Halfstuff called and again they shouted. "

"Who shouted? " asked the Sultan gloomily.

"Our men, our Germans. "

"Did my Turks shout? " asked Abdul.

"They did not. They were too busy tightening their belts and fixing their bayonets. But our generous fellows shouted for them. Then Prinz Halfstuff called out, 'The place of honour is for our Turkish brothers. Let them charge! ' And all our men shouted again. "

"And they charged? "

"They did—and were all gloriously blown up. A magnificent victory. The blowing up of the mines blocked all the ground, checked the Russians and enabled our men, by a prearranged rush, to advance backwards, taking up a new strategic—"

"Yes, yes, " said Abdul, "I know—I have read of it, alas, only too often! And they are dead! Toomuch, " he added quietly, drawing a little pouch from his girdle, "take this pouch of rubies and give them to the wives of the dead general of our division—one to each. He had, I think, but seventeen. His walk was quiet. Allah give him peace. "

"Stop, " said Von der Doppelbauch. "I will take the rubies. I myself will charge myself with the task and will myself see that I do it myself. Give me them. "

"Be it so, Toomuch, " assented the Sultan humbly. "Give them to him. "

"And now, " continued the Field-Marshal, "there is yet one other thing further still more. " He drew a roll of paper from his pocket. "Toomuch, " he said, "bring me yonder little table, with ink, quills and sand. I have here a manifesto for His Majesty to sign. "

"No, no, " cried Abdul in renewed alarm. "Not another manifesto. Not that! I signed one only last week. "

"This is a new one, " said the Field-Marshal, as he lifted the table that Toomuch had brought into place in front of the Sultan, and spread out the papers on it. "This is a better one. This is the best one yet. "

"What does it say? " said Abdul, peering at it miserably, "I can't read it. It's not in Turkish. "

"It is your last word of proud defiance to all your enemies, " said the Marshal.

"No, no, " whined Abdul. "Not defiance; they might not understand."

"Here you declare, " went on the Field-Marshal, with his big finger on the text, "your irrevocable purpose. You swear that rather than submit you will hurl yourself into the Bosphorus. "

"Where does it say that? " screamed Abdul.

"Here beside my thumb. "

"I can't do it, I can't do it, " moaned the little Sultan.

"More than that further, " went on the Prussian quite undisturbed, "you state hereby your fixed resolve, rather than give in, to cast yourself from the highest pinnacle of the topmost minaret of this palace. "

"Oh, not the highest; don't make it the highest, " moaned Abdul.

"Your purpose is fixed. Nothing can alter it. Unless the Allied Powers withdraw from their advance on Constantinople you swear that within one hour you will fill your mouth with mud and burn yourself alive. "

"Just Allah! " cried the Sultan. "Does it say all that? "

"All that, " said Von der Doppelbauch. "All that within an hour. It is a splendid defiance. The Kaiser himself has seen it and admired it. 'These, ' he said, 'are the words of a man! '"

"Did he say that? " said Abdul, evidently flattered. "And is he too about to hurl himself off his minaret? "

"For the moment, no, " replied Von der Doppelbauch sternly.

"Well, well, " said Abdul, and to my surprise he began picking up the pen and making ready. "I suppose if I must sign it, I must. " Then he marked the paper and sprinkled it with sand. "For one hour? Well, well, " he murmured. "Von der Doppelbauch Pasha, " he added with dignity, "you are permitted to withdraw. Commend me to your Imperial Master, my brother. Tell him that, when I am gone, he may have Constantinople, provided only"—and a certain slyness appeared in the Sultan's eye—"that he can get it. Farewell. "

The Field-Marshal, majestic as ever, gathered up the manifesto, clicked his heels together and withdrew.

As the door closed behind him, I had expected the little Sultan to fall into hopeless collapse.

Not at all. On the contrary, a look of peculiar cheerfulness spread over his features.

He refilled his narghileh and began quietly smoking at it.

"Toomuch, " he said, quite cheerfully, "I see there is no hope. "

"Alas! " said the secretary.

"I have now, " went on the Sultan, "apparently but sixty minutes in front of me. I had hoped that the intervention of the United States might have saved me. It has not. Instead of it, I meet my fate. Well, well, it is Kismet. I bow to it. "

He smoked away quite cheerfully.

Presently he paused.

"Toomuch, " he said, "kindly go and fetch me a sharp knife, double-edged if possible, but sharp, and a stout bowstring. "

Up to this time I had remained a mere spectator of what had happened. But now I feared that I was on the brink of witnessing an awful tragedy.

"Good heavens, Abdul, " I said, "what are you going to do? "

"Do? Why kill myself, of course, " the Sultan answered, pausing for a moment in an interval of his cheerful smoking. "What else should I do? What else is there to do? I shall first stab myself in the stomach and then throttle myself with the bowstring. In half an hour I shall be in paradise. Toomuch, summon hither from the inner harem Fatima and Falloola; they shall sit beside me and sing to me at the last hour, for I love them well, and later they too shall voyage with me to paradise. See to it that they are both thrown a little later into the Bosphorus, for my heart yearns towards the two of them, " and he added thoughtfully, "especially perhaps towards Fatima, but I have never quite made up my mind. "

The Sultan sat back with a little gurgle of contentment, the rose water bubbling soothingly in the bowl of his pipe.

Then he turned to his secretary again.

"Toomuch, " he said, "you will at the same time send a bowstring to Codfish Pasha, my Chief of War. It is our sign, you know, " he added in explanation to me—"it gives Codfish leave to kill himself. And, Toomuch, send a bowstring also to Beefhash Pasha, my Vizier— good fellow, he will expect it—and to Macpherson Effendi, my financial adviser. Let them all have bowstrings. "

"Stop, stop, " I pleaded. "I don't understand. "

"Why surely, " said the little man, in evident astonishment, "it is plain enough. What would you do in Canada? When your ministers—as I think you call them—fail and no longer enjoy your support, do you not send them bowstrings? "

"Never, " I said. "They go out of office, but—"

"And they do not disembowel themselves on their retirement? Have they not that privilege? "

"Never! " I said. "What an idea! "

"The ways of the infidel. " said the little Sultan, calmly resuming his pipe, "are beyond the compass of the true intelligence of the Faithful. Yet I thought it was so even as here. I had read in your newspapers that after your last election your ministers were buried alive—buried under a landslide, was it not? We thought it—here in Turkey—a noble fate for them. "

"They crawled out, " I said.

"Ishmillah! " ejaculated Abdul. "But go, Toomuch. And listen, thou also—for in spite of all thou hast served me well—shalt have a bowstring. "

"Oh, master, master, " cried Toomuch, falling on his knees in gratitude and clutching the sole of Abdul's slipper. "It is too kind! "

"Nay, nay, " said the Sultan. "Thou hast deserved it. And I will go further. This stranger, too, my governess, this professor, bring also for the professor a bowstring, and a two-bladed knife! All Canada shall rejoice to hear of it. The students shall leap up like young lambs at the honour that will be done. Bring the knife, Toomuch; bring the knife! "

"Abdul, " I said, "Abdul, this is too much. I refuse. I am not fit. The honour is too great. "

"Not so, " said Abdul. "I am still Sultan. I insist upon it. For, listen, I have long penetrated your disguise and your kind design. I saw it from the first. You knew all and came to die with me. It was kindly meant. But you shall die no common death; yours shall be the honour of the double knife—let it be extra sharp, Toomuch—and the bowstring. "

"Abdul, " I urged, "it cannot be. You forget. I have an appointment to be thrown into the Bosphorus. "

"The death of a dog! Never! " cried Abdul. "My will is still law. Toomuch, kill him on the spot. Hit him with the stool, throw the coffee at him—"

But at this moment there were heard loud cries and shouting as in tones of great gladness, in the outer hall of the palace, doors swinging to and fro and the sound of many running feet. One heard above all the call, "It has come! It has come! "

The Sultan looked up quickly.

"Toomuch, " he said eagerly and anxiously, "quick, see what it is. Hurry! hurry! Haste! Do not stay on ceremony. Drink a cup of coffee, give me five cents—fifty cents, anything—and take leave and see what it is. "

But before Toomuch could reply, a turbaned attendant had already burst in through the door unannounced and thrown himself at Abdul's feet.

"Master! Master! " he cried. "It is here. It has come. " As he spoke he held out in one hand a huge envelope, heavy with seals. I could detect in great letters stamped across it the words, WASHINGTON and OFFICE OF THE SECRETARY OF STATE.

Abdul seized and opened the envelope with trembling hands.

"It is it! " he cried. "It is sent by Smith Pasha, Minister under the Peace of Heaven of the United States. It is the Intervention. I am saved. "

Then there was silence among us, breathless and anxious.

Abdul glanced down the missive, reading it in silence to himself.

"Oh noble, " he murmured. "Oh generous! It is too much. Too splendid a lot! "

"What does it say? "

"Look, " said the Sultan. "The United States has used its good offices. It has intervened! All is settled. My fate is secure. "

"Yes, yes, " I said, "but what is it? "

"Is it believable? " exclaimed Abdul. "It appears that none of the belligerents cared about *me* at all. None had designs upon me. The war was *not* made, as we understood, Toomuch, as an attempt to seize my person. All they wanted was Constantinople. Not *me* at all!"

"Powerful Allah! " murmured Toomuch. "Why was it not so said? "

"For me, " said the Sultan, still consulting the letter, "great honours are prepared! I am to leave Constantinople —that is the sole condition. It shall then belong to whoever can get it. Nothing could be fairer. It always has. I am to have a safe conduct—is it not noble? —to the United States. No one is to attempt to poison me—is it not generosity itself? —neither on land nor even—mark this especially, Toomuch—on board ship. Nor is anyone to throw me overboard or otherwise transport me to paradise. "

"It passes belief! " murmured Toomuch Koffi. "Allah is indeed good."

"In the United States itself, " went on Abdul, "or, I should say, themselves, Toomuch, for are they not innumerable? I am to have a position of the highest trust, power and responsibility. "

"Is it really possible? " I said, greatly surprised.

"It is so written, " said the Sultan. "I am to be placed at the head, as the sole head or sovereign of—how is it written? —a *Turkish Bath Establishment* in New York. There I am to enjoy the same freedom and to exercise just as much—it is so written—exactly as much political power as I do here. Is it not glorious? "

"Allah! Illallah! " cried the secretary.

"You, Toomuch, shall come with me, for there is a post of great importance placed at my disposal—so it is written—under the title of Rubber Down. Toomuch, let our preparations be made at once. Notify Fatima and Falloola. Those two alone shall go, for it is a Christian country and I bow to its prejudices. Two, I understand, is the limit. But we must leave at once. "

The Sultan paused a moment and then looked at me.

"And our good friend here, " he added, "we must leave to get out of this Yildiz Kiosk by whatsoever magic means he came into it. "

Which I did.

And I am assured, by those who know, that the intervention was made good and that Abdul and Toomuch may be seen to this day, or to any other day, moving to and fro in their slippers and turbans in their Turkish Bath Emporium at the corner of Broadway and—

But stop; that would be saying too much, especially as Fatima and Falloola occupy the upstairs.

And it is said that Abdul has developed a very special talent for heating up the temperature for his Christian customers.

Further Foolishness

Moreover, it is the general opinion that, whether or not the Kaiser and such people will get their deserts, Abdul Aziz has his.

XIII. In Merry Mexico

I stood upon the platform of the little deserted railway station of the frontier and looked around at the wide prospect. "So this, " I said to myself, "is Mexico! "

About me was the great plain rolling away to the Sierras in the background. The railroad track traversed it in a thin line. There were no trees—only here and there a clump of cactus or chaparral, a tuft of dog-grass or a few patches of dogwood. At intervals in the distance one could see a hacienda standing in majestic solitude in a cup of the hills. In the blue sky floated little banderillos of white cloud, while a graceful hidalgo appeared poised on a crag on one leg with folded wings, or floated lazily in the sky on one wing with folded legs.

There was a drowsy buzzing of cicadas half asleep in the cactus cups, and, from some hidden depth of the hills far in the distance, the tinkling of a mule bell.

I had seen it all so often in moving pictures that I recognised the scene at once.

"So this is Mexico? " I repeated.

The station building beside me was little more than a wooden shack. Its door was closed. There was a sort of ticket wicket opening at the side, but it too was closed.

But as I spoke thus aloud, the wicket opened. There appeared in it the head and shoulders of a little wizened man, swarthy and with bright eyes and pearly teeth.

He wore a black velvet suit with yellow facings, and a tall straw hat running to a point. I seemed to have seen him a hundred times in comic opera.

"Can you tell me when the next train—? " I began.

The little man made a gesture of Spanish politeness.

"Welcome to Mexico! " he said.

"Could you tell me—? " I continued.

"Welcome to our sunny Mexico! " he repeated—"our beautiful, glorious Mexico. Her heart throbs at the sight of you. "

"Would you mind—? " I began again.

"Our beautiful Mexico, torn and distracted as she is, greets you. In the name of the *de facto* government, thrice welcome. *Su casa!* " he added with a graceful gesture indicating the interior of his little shack. "Come in and smoke cigarettes and sleep. *Su casa!* You are capable of Spanish, is it not? "

"No, " I said, "it is not. But I wanted to know when the next train for the interior—"

"Ah! " he rejoined more briskly. "You address me as a servant of the *de facto* government. *Momentino!* One moment! "

He shut the wicket and was gone a long time. I thought he had fallen asleep.

But he reappeared. He had a bundle of what looked like railway time tables, very ancient and worn, in his hand.

"Did you say, " he questioned, "the *in*terior or the *ex*terior? "

"The interior, please. "

"Ah, good, excellent—for the interior. " The little Mexican retreated into his shack and I could hear him murmuring, "For the interior, excellent, " as he moved to and fro.

Presently he reappeared, a look of deep sorrow on his face.

"Alas, " he said, shrugging his shoulders, "I am *desolado!* It has gone! The next train has gone! "

"Gone! When? "

"Alas, who can tell? Yesterday, last month? But it has gone. "

"And when will there be another one? " I asked.

"Ha! " he said, resuming a brisk official manner. "I understand. Having missed the next, you propose to take another one. Excellent! What business enterprise you foreigners have! You miss your train! What do you do? Do you abandon your journey? No. Do you sit down—do you weep? No. Do you lose time? You do not. "

"Excuse me, " I said, "but when is there another train? "

"That must depend, " said the little official, and as he spoke he emerged from his house and stood beside me on the platform fumbling among his railway guides. "The first question is, do you propose to take a *de facto* train or a *de jure* train? "

"When do they go? " I asked.

"There is a *de jure* train, " continued the stationmaster, peering into his papers, "at two p. m. A very good train—sleepers and diners— one at four, a through train—sleepers, observation car, dining car, corridor compartments—that also is a *de jure* train—"

"But what is the difference between the *de jure* and the *de facto*? "

"It's a distinction we generally make in Mexico. The *de jure* trains are those that ought to go; that is, in theory, they go. The *de facto* trains are those that actually do go. It is a distinction clearly established in our correspondence with Huedro Huilson. "

"Do you mean Woodrow Wilson? "

"Yes, Huedro Huilson, president—*de jure*—of the United States. "

"Oh, " I said. "Now I understand. And when will there be a *de facto* train? "

"At any moment you like, " said the little official with a bow.

"But I don't see—"

"Pardon me, I have one here behind the shed on that side track. Excuse me one moment and I will bring it. "

He disappeared and I presently saw him energetically pushing out from behind the shed a little railroad lorry or hand truck.

"Now then, " he said as he shoved his little car on to the main track, "this is the train. Seat yourself. I myself will take you. "

"And how much shall I pay? What is the fare to the interior? " I questioned.

The little man waved the idea aside with a polite gesture.

"The fare, " he said, "let us not speak of it. Let us forget it How much money have you? "

"I have here, " I said, taking out a roll of bills, "fifty dollars—"

"And that is *all* you have? "

"Yes. "

"Then let *that* be your fare! Why should I ask more? Were I an American, I might; but in our Mexico, no. What you have we take; beyond that we ask nothing. Let us forget it. Good! And, now, would you prefer to travel first, second, or third class? "

"First class please, " I said.

"Very good. Let it be so. " Here the little man took from his pocket a red label marked FIRST CLASS and tied it on the edge of the hand car. "It is more comfortable, " he said. "Now seat yourself, seize hold of these two handles in front of you. Move them back and forward, thus. Beyond that you need do nothing. The working of the car, other than the mere shoving of the handles, shall be my task. Consider yourself, in fact, *senor*, as my guest. "

We took our places. I applied myself, as directed, to the handles and the little car moved forward across the plain.

"A glorious prospect, " I said, as I gazed at the broad panorama.

"*Magnifico!* Is it not? " said my companion. "Alas, my poor Mexico! She want nothing but water to make her the most fertile country of the globe! Water and soil, those only, and she would excel all others. Give her but water, soil, light, heat, capital and labour, and what could she not be! And what do we see? Distraction, revolution,

110

destruction—pardon me, will you please stop the car a moment? I wish to tear up a little of the track behind us. "

I did as directed. My companion descended, and with a little bar that he took from beneath the car unloosed a few of the rails of the light track and laid them beside the road.

"It is our custom, " he explained, as he climbed on board again. "We Mexicans, when we move to and fro, always tear up the track behind us. But what was I saying? Ah, yes—destruction, desolation, alas, our Mexico! "

He looked sadly up at the sky.

"You speak, " I said, "like a patriot. May I ask your name? "

"My name is Raymon, " he answered, with a bow, "Raymon Domenico y Miraflores de las Gracias. "

"And may I call you simply Raymon? "

"I shall be delirious with pleasure if you will do so, " he answered, "and dare I ask you, in return, your business in our beautiful country? "

The car, as we were speaking, had entered upon a long gentle down-grade across the plain, so that it ran without great effort on my part.

"Certainly, " I said. "I'm going into the interior to see General Villa!"

At the shock of the name, Raymon nearly fell off the car.

"Villa! General Francesco Villa! It is not possible! "

The little man was shivering with evident fear.

"See him! See Villa! Not possible. Let me show you a picture of him instead? But approach him—it is not possible. He shoots everybody at sight! "

"That's all right, " I said. "I have a written safe conduct that protects me. "

"From whom? "

"Here, " I said, "look at them—I have two. "

Raymon took the documents I gave him and read aloud:

"'The bearer is on an important mission connected with American rights in Mexico. If anyone shoots him he will be held to a strict accountability. W. W. ' Ah! Excellent! He will be compelled to send in an itemised account. Excellent! And this other, let me see. 'If anybody interferes with the bearer, I will knock his face in. T. R. ' Admirable. This is, if anything, better than the other for use in our country. It appeals to our quick Mexican natures. It is, as we say, *simpatico*. It touches us. "

"It is meant to, " I said.

"And may I ask, " said Raymon, "the nature of your business with Villa? "

"We are old friends, " I answered. "I used to know him years ago when he kept a Mexican cigar store in Buffalo. It occurred to me that I might be able to help the cause of peaceful intervention. I have already had a certain experience in Turkey. I am commissioned to make General Villa an offer. "

"I see, " said Raymon. "In that case, if we are to find Villa let us make all haste forward. And first we must direct ourselves yonder"—he pointed in a vague way towards the mountains—"where we must presently leave our car and go on foot, to the camp of General Carranza. "

"Carranza! " I exclaimed. "But he is fighting Villa! "

"Exactly. It is *possible*—not certain—but possible, that he knows where Villa is. In our Mexico when two of our generalistas are fighting in the mountains, they keep coming across one another. It is hard to avoid it. "

"Good, " I said. "Let us go forward. "

It was two days later that we reached Carranza's camp in the mountains.

Further Foolishness

We found him just at dusk seated at a little table beneath a tree.

His followers were all about, picketing their horses and lighting fires.

The General, buried in a book before him, noticed neither the movements of his own men nor our approach.

I must say that I was surprised beyond measure at his appearance.

The popular idea of General Carranza as a rude bandit chief is entirely erroneous.

I saw before me a quiet, scholarly-looking man, bearing every mark of culture and refinement. His head was bowed over the book in front of him, which I noticed with astonishment and admiration was *Todhunter's Algebra*. Close at his hand I observed a work on *Decimal Fractions*, while, from time to time, I saw the General lift his eyes and glance keenly at a multiplication table that hung on a bough beside him.

"You must wait a few moments, " said an aide-de-camp, who stood beside us. "The General is at work on a simultaneous equation! "

"Is it possible? " I said in astonishment.

The aide-de-camp smiled.

"Soldiering to-day, my dear Senor, " he said, "is an exact science. On this equation will depend our entire food supply for the next week. "

"When will he get it done? " I asked anxiously.

"Simultaneously, " said the aide-de-camp.

The General looked up at this moment and saw us.

"Well? " he asked.

"Your Excellency, " said the aide-de-camp, "there is a stranger here on a visit of investigation to Mexico. "

"Shoot him! " said the General, and turned quickly to his work.

The aide-de-camp saluted.

"When? " he asked.

"As soon as he likes, " said the General.

"You are fortunate, indeed, " said the aide-de-camp, in a tone of animation, as he led me away, still accompanied by Raymon. "You might have been kept waiting round for days. Let us get ready at once. You would like to be shot, would you not, smoking a cigarette, and standing beside your grave? Luckily, we have one ready. Now, if you will wait a moment, I will bring the photographer and his machine. There is still light enough, I think. What would you like it called? *The Fate of a Spy?* That's good, isn't it? Our syndicate can always work up that into a two-reel film. All the rest of it—the camp, the mountains, the general, the funeral and so on—we can do to-morrow without you. "

He was all eagerness as he spoke.

"One moment, " I interrupted. "I am sure there is some mistake. I only wished to present certain papers and get a safe conduct from the General to go and see Villa. "

The aide-de-camp stopped abruptly.

"Ah! " he said. "You are not here for a picture. A thousand pardons. Give me your papers. One moment—I will return to the General and explain. "

He vanished, and Raymon and I waited in the growing dusk.

"No doubt the General supposed, " explained Raymon, as he lighted a cigarette, "that you were here for *las machinas*, the moving pictures."

In a few minutes the aide-de-camp returned.

"Come, " he said, "the General will see you now. "

We returned to where we had left Carranza.

The General rose to meet me with outstretched hand and with a gesture of simple cordiality.

"You must pardon my error, " he said.

"Not at all, " I said.

"It appears you do not desire to be shot. "

"Not at present. "

"Later, perhaps, " said the General. "On your return, no doubt, provided, " he added with grave courtesy that sat well on him, "that you do return. My aide-de-camp shall make a note of it. But at present you wish to be guided to Francesco Villa? "

"If it is possible. "

"Quite easy. He is at present near here, in fact much nearer than he has any right to be. " The General frowned. "We found this spot first. The light is excellent and the mountains, as you have seen, are wonderful for our pictures. This is, by every rule of decency, *our* scenery. Villa has no right to it. This is *our* Revolution" —the General spoke with rising animation— "not his. When you see the fellow, tell him from me—or tell his manager—that he must either move his revolution further away or, by heaven, I'll—I'll use force against him. But stop, " he checked himself. "You wish to see Villa. Good. You have only to follow the straight track over the mountain there. He is just beyond, at the little village in the hollow, El Corazon de las Quertas. "

The General shook hands and seated himself again at his work. The interview was at an end. We withdrew.

The next morning we followed without difficulty the path indicated. A few hours' walk over the mountain pass brought us to a little straggling village of adobe houses, sleeping drowsily in the sun.

There were but few signs of life in its one street—a mule here and there tethered in the sun, and one or two Mexicans drowsily smoking in the shade.

One building only, evidently newly made, and of lumber, had a decidedly American appearance. Its doorway bore the sign GENERAL OFFICES OF THE COMPANY, and under it the notice KEEP OUT, while on one of its windows was painted GENERAL MANAGER and below it the legend NO ADMISSION, and on the other, SECRETARY'S OFFICE: GO AWAY.

We therefore entered at once.

"General Francesco Villa? " said a clerk, evidently American. "Yes, he's here all right. At least, this is the office. "

"And where is the General? " I asked.

The clerk turned to an assistant at a desk in a corner of the room.

"Where's Frank working this morning? " he asked.

"Over down in the gulch, " said the other, turning round for a moment. "There's an attack on American cavalry this morning. "

"Oh, yes, I forgot, " said the chief clerk. "I thought it was the Indian Massacre, but I guess that's for to-morrow. Go straight to the end of the street and turn left about half a mile and you'll find the boys down there. "

We thanked him and withdrew.

We passed across the open plaza, and went down a narrow side road, bordered here and there with adobe houses, and so out into the open country. Here the hills rose again and the road that we followed wound sharply round a turn into a deep gorge, bordered with rocks and sage brush. We had no sooner turned the curve of the road than we came upon a scene of great activity. Men in Mexican costume were running to and fro apparently arranging a sort of barricade at the side of the road. Others seemed to be climbing the rocks on the further side of the gorge, as if seeking points of advantage. I noticed that all were armed with rifles and machetes and presented a formidable appearance. Of Villa himself I could see nothing. But there was a grim reality about the glittering knives, the rifles and the maxim guns that I saw concealed in the sage brush beside the road.

"What is it? " I asked of a man who was standing idle, watching the scene from the same side of the road as ourselves.

"Attack of American cavalry, " he said nonchalantly.

"Here! " I gasped.

"Yep, in about ten minutes: soon as they are ready. "

"Where's Villa? "

"It's him they're attacking. They chase him here, see! This is an ambush. Villa rounds on them right here, and they fight to a finish! "

"Great heavens! " I exclaimed. "How do you know that? "

"Know it? Why because I *seen* it. Ain't they been trying it out for three days? Why, I'd be in it myself only I'm off work. Got a sore toe yesterday—horse stepped on it. "

All this was, of course, quite unintelligible to me.

"But it's right here where they're going to fight? " I asked.

"Sure, " said the American, as he moved carelessly aside, "as soon as the boss gets it all ready. "

I noticed for the first time a heavy-looking man in an American tweed suit and a white plug hat, moving to and fro and calling out directions with an air of authority.

"Here! " he shouted, "what in h—l are you doing with that machine gun? You've got it clean out of focus. Here, Jose, come in closer—that's right. Steady there now, and don't forget, at the second whistle you and Pete are dead. Here, you, Pete, how in thunder do you think you can die there? You're all out of the picture and hidden by that there sage brush. That's no place to die. And, boys, remember one thing, now, *die slow*. Ed"—he turned and called apparently to some one invisible behind the rocks—"when them two boys is killed, turn her round on them, slew her round good and get them centre focus. Now then, are you all set? Ready? "

At this moment the speaker turned and saw Raymon and myself.

"Here, youse, " he shouted, "get further back, you're in the picture. Or, say, no, stay right where you are. You, " he said, pointing to me, "stay right where you are and I'll give you a dollar to just hold that horror; you understand, just keep on registering it. Don't do another thing, just register that face. "

His words were meaningless to me. I had never known before that it was possible to make money by merely registering my face.

"No, no, " cried out Raymon, "my friend here is not wanting work. He has a message, a message of great importance for General Villa. "

"Well, " called back the boss, "he'll have to wait. We can't stop now. All ready, boys? One—two—now! "

And with that he put a whistle to his lips and blew a long shrill blast.

Then in a moment the whole scene was transformed. Rifle shots rang out from every crag and bush that bordered the gully.

A wild scamper of horses' hoofs was heard and in a moment there came tearing down the road a whole troop of mounted Mexicans, evidently in flight, for they turned and fired from their saddles as they rode. The horses that carried them were wild with excitement and flecked with foam. The Mexican cavalry men shouted and yelled, brandishing their machetes and firing their revolvers. Here and there a horse and rider fell to the ground in a great whirl of sand and dust. In the thick of the press, a leader of ferocious aspect, mounted upon a gigantic black horse, waved his sombrero about his head.

"Villa—it is Villa! " cried Raymon, tense with excitement. "Is he not *magnifico?* But look! Look—the *Americanos!* They are coming! "

It was a glorious sight to see them as they rode madly on the heels of the Mexicans—a whole company of American cavalry, their horses shoulder to shoulder, the men bent low in their saddles, their carbines gripped in their hands. They rode in squadrons and in line, not like the shouting, confused mass of the Mexicans—but steady, disciplined, irresistible.

On the right flank in front a grey-haired officer steadied the charging line. The excitement of it was maddening.

"Go to it, " I shouted in uncontrollable emotion. "Your Mexicans are licked, Raymon, they're no good! "

"But look! " said Raymon. "See—the ambush, the ambuscada! "

For as they reached the centre of the gorge in front of us the Mexicans suddenly checked their horses, bringing them plunging on their haunches in the dust, and then swung round upon their pursuers, while from every crag and bush at the side of the gorge the concealed riflemen sprang into view—and the sputtering of the machine guns swept the advancing column with a volley.

We could see the American line checked as with the buffet of a great wave, men and horses rolling in the road. Through the smoke one saw the grey-haired leader —dismounted, his uniform torn, his hat gone, but still brandishing his sword and calling his orders to his men, his face as one caught in a flash of sunlight, steady and fearless. His words I could not hear, but one saw the American cavalry, still unbroken, dismount, throw themselves behind their horses, and fire with steady aim into the mass of the Mexicans. We could see the Mexicans in front of where we stood falling thick and fast, in little huddled bundles of colour, kicking the sand. The man Pete had gone down right in the foreground and was breathing out his soul before our eyes.

"Well done, " I shouted. "Go to it, boys! You can lick 'em yet! Hurrah for the United States. Look, Raymon, look! They've shot down the crew of the machine guns. See, see, the Mexicans are turning to run. At 'em, boys! They're waving the American flag! There it is in all the thick of the smoke! Hark! There's the bugle call to mount again! They're going to charge again! Here they come! "

As the American cavalry came tearing forward, the Mexicans leaped from their places with gestures of mingled rage and terror as if about to break and run.

The battle, had it continued, could have but one end.

But at this moment we heard from the town behind us the long sustained note of a steam whistle blowing the hour of noon.

In an instant the firing ceased.

Further Foolishness

The battle stopped. The Mexicans picked themselves up off the ground and began brushing off the dust from their black velvet jackets. The American cavalry reined in their horses. Dead Pete came to life. General Villa and the American leader and a number of others strolled over towards the boss, who stood beside the fence vociferating his comments.

"That won't do! " he was shouting. "That won't do! Where in blazes was that infernal Sister of Mercy? Miss Jenkinson! " and he called to a tall girl, whom I now noticed for the first time among the crowd, wearing a sort of khaki costume and a short skirt and carrying a water bottle in a strap. "You never got into the picture at all. I want you right in there among the horses, under their feet. "

"Land sakes! " said the Sister of Mercy. "You ain't no right to ask me to go in there among them horses and be trampled. "

"Ain't you *paid* to be trampled? " said the manager angrily. Then as he caught sight of Villa he broke off and said: "Frank, you boys done fine. It's going to be a good act, all right. But it ain't just got the right amount of ginger in it yet. We'll try her over *once* again, anyway. "

"Now, boys, " he continued, calling out to the crowd with a voice like a megaphone, "this afternoon at three-thirty —Hospital scene. I only want the wounded, the doctors and the Sisters of Mercy. All the rest of youse is free till ten to-morrow—for the Indian Massacre. Everybody up for that. "

It was an hour or two later that I had my interview with Villa in a back room of the little *posada*, or inn, of the town. The General had removed his ferocious wig of straight black hair, and substituted a check suit for his warlike costume. He had washed the darker part of the paint off his face—in fact, he looked once again the same Frank Villa that I used to know when he kept his Mexican cigar store in Buffalo.

"Well, Frank, " I said, "I'm afraid I came down here under a misunderstanding. "

"Looks like it, " said the General, as he rolled a cigarette.

"And you wouldn't care to go back even for the offer that I am commissioned to make—your old job back again, and half the profits on a new cigar to be called the Francesco Villa? "

The General shook his head.

"It sounds good, all right, " he said, "but this moving-picture business is better. "

"I see, " I said, "I hadn't understood. I thought there really was a revolution here in Mexico. "

"No, " said Villa, shaking his head, "been no revolution down here for years—not since Diaz. The picture companies came in and took the whole thing over; they made us a fair offer—so much a reel straight out, and a royalty, and let us divide up the territory as we liked. The first film we done was the bombardment of Vera Cruz. Say, that was a dandy; did you see it? "

"No, " I said.

"They had us all in that, " he continued. "I done an American Marine. Lots of people think it all real when they see it. "

"Why, " I said, "nearly everybody does. Even the President—"

"Oh, I guess he knows, " said Villa, "but, you see, there's tons of money in it and it's good for business, and he's too decent a man to give It away. Say, I heard the boy saying there's a war in Europe. I wonder what company got that up, eh? But I don't believe it'll draw. There ain't the scenery for it that we have in Mexico. "

"Alas! " murmured Raymon. "Our beautiful Mexico. To what is she fallen! Needing only water, air, light and soil to make her—"

"Come on, Raymon, " I said, "let's go home. "

XIV. Over the Grape Juice; or, The Peacemakers

Characters

MR. W. JENNINGS BRYAN.
DR. DAVID STARR JORDAN.
A PHILANTHROPIST.
MR. NORMAN ANGELL.
A LADY PACIFIST.
A NEGRO PRESIDENT.
AN EMINENT DIVINE.
THE MAN ON THE STREET.
THE GENERAL PUBLIC.
And many others.

"War, " said the Negro President of Haiti, "is a sad spectacle. It shames our polite civilisation. "

As he spoke, he looked about him at the assembled company around the huge dinner table, glittering with cut glass and white linen, and brilliant with hot-house flowers.

"A sad spectacle, " he repeated, rolling his big eyes in his black and yellow face that was melancholy with the broken pathos of the African race.

The occasion was a notable one. It was the banquet of the Peacemakers' Conference of 1917 and the company gathered about the board was as notable as it was numerous.

At the head of the table the genial Mr. Jennings Bryan presided as host, his broad countenance beaming with amiability, and a tall flagon of grape juice standing beside his hand. A little further down the table one saw the benevolent head and placid physiognomy of Mr. Norman Angell, bowed forward as if in deep calculation. Within earshot of Mr. Bryan, but not listening to him, one recognised without the slightest difficulty Dr. David Starr Jordan, the distinguished ichthyologist and director in chief of the World's Peace Foundation, while the bland features of a gentleman from China, and the presence of a yellow delegate from the Mosquito Coast, gave ample evidence that the company had been gathered together without reference to colour, race, religion, education, or other prejudices whatsoever.

But it would be out of the question to indicate by name the whole of the notable assemblage. Indeed, certain of the guests, while carrying in their faces and attitudes something strangely and elusively familiar, seemed in a sense to be nameless, and to represent rather types and abstractions than actual personalities. Such was the case, for instance, with a female member of the company, seated in a place of honour near the host, whose demure garb and gentle countenance seemed to indicate her as a Lady Pacifist, but denied all further identification. The mild, ecclesiastical features of a second guest, so entirely Christian in its expression as to be almost devoid of expression altogether, marked him at once as An Eminent Divine, but, while puzzlingly suggestive of an actual and well-known person, seemed to elude exact recognition. His accent, when he presently spoke, stamped him as British and his garb was that of the Established Church. Another guest appeared to answer to the general designation of Capitalist or Philanthropist, and seemed from his prehensile grasp upon his knife and fork to typify the Money Power. In front of this guest, doubtless with a view of indicating his extreme wealth and the consideration in which he stood, was placed a floral decoration representing a broken bank, with the figure of a ruined depositor entwined among the debris.

Of these nameless guests, two individuals alone, from the very significance of their appearance, from their plain dress, unsuited to the occasion, and from the puzzled expression of their faces, seemed out of harmony with the galaxy of distinction which surrounded them. They seemed to speak only to one another, and even that somewhat after the fashion of an appreciative chorus to what the rest of the company was saying; while the manner in which they rubbed their hands together and hung upon the words of the other speakers in humble expectancy seemed to imply that they were present in the hope of gathering rather than shedding light. To these two humble and obsequious guests no attention whatever was paid, though it was understood, by those who knew, that their names were The General Public and the Man on the Street.

"A sad spectacle, " said the Negro President, and he sighed as he spoke. "One wonders if our civilisation, if our moral standards themselves, are slipping from us. " Then half in reverie, or as if overcome by the melancholy of his own thought, he lifted a spoon from the table and slid it gently into the bosom of his faded uniform.

"Put back that spoon! " called The Lady Pacifist sharply.

"Pardon! " said the Negro President humbly, as he put it back. The humiliation of generations of servitude was in his voice.

"Come, come, " exclaimed Mr. Jennings Bryan cheerfully, "try a little more of the grape juice? "

"Does it intoxicate? " asked the President.

"Never, " answered Mr. Bryan. "Rest assured of that. I can guarantee it. The grape is picked in the dark. It is then carried, still in the dark, to the testing room. There every particle of alcohol is removed. Try it. "

"Thank you, " said the President. "I am no longer thirsty. "

"Will anybody have some more of the grape juice? " asked Mr. Bryan, running his eye along the ranks of the guests.

No one spoke.

"Will anybody have some more ground peanuts? "

No one moved.

"Or does anybody want any more of the shredded tan bark? No? Or will somebody have another spoonful of sunflower seeds? "

There was still no sign of assent.

"Very well, then, " said Mr. Bryan, "the banquet, as such, is over, and we now come to the more serious part of our business. I need hardly tell you that we are here for a serious purpose. We are here to do good. That I know is enough to enlist the ardent sympathy of everybody present. "

There was a murmur of assent.

"Personally, " said The Lady Pacifist, "I do nothing else. "

"Neither do I, " said the guest who has been designated The Philanthropist, "whether I am producing oil, or making steel, or building motor-cars. "

"Does he build motor-cars? " whispered the humble person called The Man in the Street to his fellow, The General Public.

"All great philanthropists do things like that, " answered his friend. "They do it as a social service so as to benefit humanity; any money they make is just an accident. They don't really care about it a bit. Listen to him. He's going to say so. "

"Indeed, our business itself, " The Philanthropist continued, while his face lighted up with unselfish enthusiasm, "our business itself—"

"Hush, hush! " said Mr. Bryan gently. "We know—"

"Our business itself, " persisted The Philanthropist, "is one great piece of philanthropy. "

Tears gathered in his eyes.

"Come, come, " said Mr. Bryan firmly, "we must get to business. Our friend here, " he continued, turning to the company at large and indicating the Negro President on his right, "has come to us in great distress. His beautiful island of Haiti is and has been for many years overwhelmed in civil war. Now he learns that not only Haiti, but also Europe is engulfed in conflict. He has heard that we are making proposals for ending the war —indeed, I may say are about to declare that the war in Europe *must stop*—I think I am right, am I not, my friends? "

There was a general chorus of assent.

"Naturally then, " continued Mr. Bryan, "our friend the President of Haiti, who is overwhelmed with grief at what has been happening in his island, has come to us for help. That is correct, is it not? "

"That's it, gentlemen, " said the Negro President, in a voice of some emotion, wiping the sleeve of his faded uniform across his eyes. "The situation is quite beyond my control. In fact, " he added, shaking his head pathetically as he relapsed into more natural speech, "dis hyah chile, gen'l'n, is clean done beat with it. Dey ain't doin' nuffin' on the island but shootin', burnin', and killin' somethin' awful. Lawd a massy! it's just like a real civilised country, all right, now. Down in our island we coloured people is feeling just as bad as youse did when all them poor white folks was murdered on the *Lusitania!* "

But the Negro President had no sooner used the words "Murdered on the *Lusitania*, " than a chorus of dissent and disapproval broke out all down the table.

"My dear sir, my dear sir, " protested Mr. Bryan, "pray moderate your language a little, if you please. Murdered? Oh, dear, dear me, how can we hope to advance the cause of peace if you insist on using such terms? "

"Ain't it that? Wasn't it murder? " asked the President, perplexed.

"We are all agreed here, " said The Lady Pacifist, "that it is far better to call it an incident. We speak of the '*Lusitania* Incident, '" she added didactically, "just as one speaks of the *Arabic* Incident, and the Cavell Incident, and other episodes of the sort. It makes it so much easier to forget. "

"True, quite true, " murmured The Eminent Divine, "and then one must remember that there are always two sides to everything. There are two sides to murder. We must not let ourselves forget that there is always the murderer's point of view to consider. "

But by this time the Negro President was obviously confused and out of his depth. The conversation had reached a plane of civilisation which was beyond his reach.

The genial Mr. Bryan saw fit to come to his rescue.

"Never mind, " said Mr. Bryan soothingly. "Our friends here, will soon settle all your difficulties for you. I'm going to ask them, one after the other, to advise you. They will tell you the various means that they are about to apply to stop the war in Europe, and you may select any that you like for your use in Haiti. We charge you nothing for it, except of course your fair share of the price of this grape juice and the shredded nuts. "

The President nodded.

"I am going to ask our friend on my right"—and here Mr. Bryan indicated The Lady Pacifist—"to speak first. "

There was a movement of general expectancy and the two obsequious guests at the foot of the table, of whom mention has been made, were seen to nudge one another and whisper, "Isn't this splendid? "

"You are not asking me to speak first merely because I am a woman?" asked The Lady Pacifist.

"Oh no, " said Mr. Bryon, with charming tact.

"Very good, " said the lady, adjusting her glasses. "As for stopping the war, I warn you, as I have warned the whole world, that it may be too late. They should have called me in sooner. That was the mistake. If they had sent for me at once and had put my picture in the papers both in England and Germany, with the inscription 'The True Woman of To-day, ' I doubt if any of the men who looked at it would have felt that it was worth while to fight. But, as things are, the only advice I can give is this. Everybody is wrong (except me). The Germans are a very naughty people. But the Belgians are worse. It was very, very wicked of the Germans to bombard the houses of the Belgians. But how naughty of the Belgians to go and sit in their houses while they were bombarded. It is to that that I attribute—with my infallible sense of justice—the dreadful loss of life. So you see the only conclusion that I can reach is that everybody is very naughty and that the only remedy would be to appoint me a committee—me and a few others, though the others don't really matter—to make a proper settlement. I hope I make myself clear. "

The Negro President shook his head and looked mystified.

"Us coloured folks, " he said, "wouldn't quite understand that. We done got the idea that sometimes there's such a thing as a quarrel that is right and just. " The President's melancholy face lit up with animation and his voice rose to the sonorous vibration of the negro preacher. "We learn that out of the Bible, we coloured folks—we learn to smite the ungodly—"

"Pray, pray, " said Mr. Bryan soothingly, "don't introduce religion, let me beg of you. That would be fatal. We peacemakers are all agreed that there must be no question of religion raised. "

"Exactly so, " murmured The Eminent Divine, "my own feelings exactly. The name of—of—the Deity should never be brought in. It inflames people. Only a few weeks ago I was pained and grieved to the heart to hear a woman in one of our London streets raving that the German Emperor was a murderer. Her child had been killed that night by a bomb from a Zeppelin; she had its body in a cloth hugged to her breast as she talked—thank heaven, they keep these things out of the newspapers—and she was calling down God's vengeance on the Emperor. Most deplorable! Poor creature, unable, I suppose, to realise the Emperor's exalted situation, his splendid lineage, the wonderful talent with which he can draw pictures of the apostles with one hand while he writes an appeal to his Mohammedan comrades with the other. I dined with him once, " he added, in modest afterthought.

"I dined with him, too, " said Dr. Jordan. "I shall never forget the impression he made. As he entered the room accompanied by his staff, the Emperor looked straight at me and said to one of his aides, 'Who is this? ' 'This is Dr. Jordan, ' said the officer. The Emperor put out his hand. 'So this is Dr. Jordan, ' he said. I never witnessed such an exhibition of brain power in my life. He had seized my name in a moment and held it for three seconds with all the tenaciousness of a Hohenzollern.

"But may I, " continued the Director of the World's Peace, "add a word to what has been said to make it still clearer to our friend? I will try to make it as simple as one of my lectures in Ichthyology. I know of nothing simpler than that. "

Everybody murmured assent. The Negro President put his hand to his ear.

"Theology? " he said.

"Ichthyology, " said Dr. Jordan. "It is better. But just listen to this. War is waste. It destroys the tissues. It is exhausting and fatiguing and may in extreme cases lead to death. "

The learned gentleman sat back in his seat and took a refreshing drink of rain water from a glass beside him, while a murmur of applause ran round the table. It was known and recognised that the speaker had done more than any living man to establish the fact that war is dangerous, that gunpowder, if heated, explodes, that fire burns, that fish swim, and other great truths without which the work of the peace endowment would appear futile.

"And now, " said Mr. Bryan, looking about him with the air of a successful toastmaster, "I am going to ask our friend here to give us his views. "

Renewed applause bore witness to the popularity of The Philanthropist, whom Mr. Bryan had indicated with a wave of his hand.

The Philanthropist cleared his throat.

"In our business—" he began.

Mr. Bryan plucked him gently by the sleeve.

"Never mind your business just now, " he whispered.

The Philanthropist bowed in assent and continued:

"I will come at once to the subject. My own feeling is that the true way to end war is to try to spread abroad in all directions goodwill and brotherly love. "

"Hear, hear! " cried the assembled company.

"And the great way to inspire brotherly love all round is to keep on getting richer and richer till you have so much money that every one loves you. Money, gentlemen, is a glorious thing. "

At this point, Mr. Norman Angell, who had remained silent hitherto, raised his head from his chest and murmured drowsily:

"Money, money, there isn't anything but money. Money is the only thing there is. Money and property, property and money. If you destroy it, it is gone; if you smash it, it isn't there. All the rest is a great illus—"

And with this he dozed off again into silence.

"Our poor Angell is asleep again, " said The Lady Pacifist.

Mr. Bryan shook his head.

"He's been that way ever since the war began—sleeps all the time, and keeps muttering that there isn't any war, that people only imagine it, in fact that it is all an illusion. But I fear we are interrupting you, " he added, turning to The Philanthropist.

"I was just saying, " continued that gentleman, "that you can do anything with money. You can stop a war with it if you have enough of it, in ten minutes. I don't care what kind of war it is, or what the people are fighting for, whether they are fighting for conquest or fighting for their homes and their children. I can stop it, stop it absolutely by my grip on money, without firing a shot or incurring the slightest personal danger. "

The Philanthropist spoke with the greatest emphasis, reaching out his hand and clutching his fingers in the air.

"Yes, gentlemen, " he went on, "I am speaking here not of theories but of facts. This is what I am doing and what I mean to do. You've no idea how amenable people are, especially poor people, struggling people, those with ties and responsibilities, to the grip of money. I went the other day to a man I know, the head of a bank, where I keep a little money—just a fraction of what I make, gentlemen, a mere nothing to me but everything to this man because he is still not rich and is only fighting his way up. 'Now, ' I said to him, 'you are English, are you not? ' 'Yes, sir, ' he answered. 'And I understand you mean to help along the loan to England with all the power of your bank. ' 'Yes, ' he said, 'I mean it and I'll do it. ' 'Then I'll tell you what, ' I said, 'you lend one penny, or help to lend one penny, to the people of England or the people of France, and I'll break you, I'll grind you into poverty—you and your wife and children and all that belongs to you. '"

The Philanthropist had spoken with so great an intensity that there was a deep stillness over the assembled company. The Negro President had straightened up in his seat, and as he looked at the speaker there was something in his erect back and his stern face and the set of his faded uniform that somehow turned him, African though he was, into a soldier.

"Sir, " he said, with his eye riveted on the speaker's face, "what happened to that banker man? "

"The fool! " said The Philanthropist. "He wouldn't hear —he defied me—he said that there wasn't money enough in all my business to buy the soul of a single Englishman. I had his directors turn him from his bank that day, and he's enlisted, the scoundrel, and is gone to the war. But his wife and family are left behind; they shall learn what the grip of the money power is—learn it in misery and poverty."

"My good sir, " said the Negro President slowly and impressively, "do you know why your plan of stopping war wouldn't work in Haiti? "

"No, " said The Philanthropist.

"Because our black people there would kill you. Whichever side they were on, whatever they thought of the war, they would take a man like you and lead you out into the town square, and stand you up against the side of an adobe house, and they'd shoot you. Come down to Haiti, if you doubt my words, and try it. "

"Thank you, " said The Philanthropist, resuming his customary manner of undisturbed gentleness, "I don't think I will. I don't think somehow that I could do business in Haiti. "

The passage at arms between the Negro President and The Philanthropist had thrown a certain confusion into the hitherto agreeable gathering. Even The Eminent Divine was seen to be slowly shaking his head from side to side, an extreme mark of excitement which he never permitted himself except under stress of passion. The two humble guests at the foot of the table were visibly perturbed. "Say, I don't like that about the banker, " squeaked one of them. "That ain't right, eh what? I don't like it. "

Mr. Bryan was aware that the meeting was in danger of serious disorder. He rapped loudly on the table for attention. When he had at last obtained silence, he spoke.

"I have kept my own views to the last, " he said, "because I cannot but feel that they possess a peculiar importance. There is, my dear friends, every prospect that within a measurable distance of time I shall be able to put them into practice. I am glad to be able to announce to you the practical certainty that four years from now I shall be President of the United States. "

At this announcement the entire company broke into spontaneous and heartfelt applause. It had long been felt by all present that Mr. Bryan was certain to be President of the United States if only he ran for the office often enough, but that the glad moment had actually arrived seemed almost too good for belief.

"Yes, my friends, " continued the genial host, "I have just had a communication from my dear friend Wilson, in which he tells me that he, himself, will never contest the office again. The Presidency, he says, interfered too much with his private life. In fact, I am authorised to state in confidence that his wife forbids him to run. "

"But, my dear Jennings, " interposed Dr. Jordan thoughtfully, "what about Mr. Hughes and Colonel Roosevelt? "

"In that quarter my certainty in the matter is absolute. I have calculated it out mathematically that I am bound to obtain, in view of my known principles, the entire German vote—which carries with it all the great breweries of the country—the whole Austrian vote, all the Hungarians of the sugar refineries, the Turks; in fact, my friends, I am positive that Roosevelt, if he dares to run, will carry nothing but the American vote! "

Loud applause greeted this announcement.

"And now let me explain my plan, which I believe is shared by a great number of sane, and other, pacifists in the country. All the great nations of the world will be invited to form a single international force consisting of a fleet so powerful and so well equipped that no single nation will dare to bid it defiance. "

Mr. Bryan looked about him with a glance of something like triumph. The whole company, and especially the Negro President, were now evidently interested. "Say, " whispered The General Public to his companion, "this sounds like the real thing? Eh, what? Isn't he a peach of a thinker? "

"What flag will your fleet fly? " asked the Negro President.

"The flags of all nations, " said Mr. Bryan.

"Where will you get your sailors? "

"From all the nations, " said Mr. Bryan, "but the uniform will be all the same, a plain white blouse with blue insertions, and white duck trousers with the word PEACE stamped across the back of them in big letters. This will help to impress the sailors with the almost sacred character of their functions. "

"But what will the fleet's functions be? " asked the President.

"Whenever a quarrel arises, " explained Mr. Bryan, "it will be submitted to a Board. Who will be on this Board, in addition to myself, I cannot as yet say. But it's of no consequence. Whenever a case is submitted to the Board it will think it over for three years. It will then announce its decision—if any. After that, if any one nation refuses to submit, its ports will be bombarded by the Peace Fleet. "

Rapturous expressions of approval greeted Mr. Bryan's explanation.

"But I don't understand, " said the Negro President, turning his puzzled face to Mr. Bryan. "Would some of these ships be British ships? "

"Oh, certainly. In view of the dominant size of the British Navy about one-quarter of all the ships would be British ships. "

"And the sailors British sailors? "

"Oh, yes, " said Mr. Bryan, "except that they would be wearing international breeches—a most important point. "

"And if the Board, made up of all sorts of people, were to give a decision against England, then these ships—British ships with British sailors—would be sent to bombard England itself. "

"Exactly, " said Mr. Bryan. "Isn't it beautifully simple? And to guarantee its working properly, " he continued, "just in case we have to use the fleet against England, we're going to ask Admiral Jellicoe himself to take command. "

The Negro President slowly shook his head.

"Marse Bryan, " he said, "you notice what I say. I know Marse Jellicoe. I done seen him lots of times when he was just a lieutenant, down in the harbour of Port au Prince. If youse folks put up this proposition to Marse Jellicoe, he'll just tell the whole lot of you to go plumb to—"

But the close of the sentence was lost by a sudden interruption. A servant entered with a folded telegram in his hand.

"For me? " said Mr. Bryan, with a winning smile.

"For the President of Haiti, sir, " said the man.

The President took the telegram and opened it clumsily with his finger and thumb amid a general silence. Then he took from his pocket and adjusted a huge pair of spectacles with a horn rim and began to read.

"Well, I 'clare to goodness! " he said.

"Who is it from? " said Mr. Bryan. "Is it anything about me? "

The Negro President shook his head.

"It's from Haiti, " he said, "from my military secretary. "

"Read it, read it, " cried the company.

"Come back home right away, " read out the Negro President, word by word. *"Everything is all right again. Joint British and American Naval Squadron came into harbour yesterday, landed fifty bluejackets and one midshipman. Perfect order. Banks open. Bars open. Mule cars all running again. Things fine. Going to have big dance at your palace. Come right back."*

The Negro President paused.

"Gentlemen, " he said, in a voice of great and deep relief, "this lets me out. I guess I won't stay for the rest of the discussion. I'll start for Haiti. I reckon there's something in this Armed Force business after all. "

XV. The White House from Without In

Being Extracts from the Diary of a President of the United States.

MONDAY. Rose early. Swept out the White House. Cooked breakfast. Prayers. Sat in the garden reading my book on Congressional Government. What a wonderful thing it is! Why doesn't Congress live up to it? Certainly a lovely morning. Sat for some time thinking how beautiful the world is. I defy anyone to make a better. Afterwards determined to utter this defiance publicly and fearlessly. Shall put in list of fearless defiances for July speeches. Shall probably use it in Oklahoma.

9.30 a. m. Bad news. British ship *Torpid* torpedoed by a torpedo. Tense atmosphere all over Washington. Retreated instantly to the pigeon-house and shut the door. I must *think*. At all costs. And no one shall hurry me.

10 a. m. Have thought. Came out of pigeon-house. It is all right. I wonder I didn't think of it sooner. The point is perfectly simple. If Admiral Tirpitz torpedoed the *Torpid* with a torpedo, Where's the torpedo Admiral Tirpitz torped? In other words, how do they know it's a torpedo? The idea seems absolutely overwhelming. Wrote notes at once to England and to Germany.

11 a. m. Gave out my idea to the Ass Press. Tense feeling at Washington vanished instantly and utterly. Feeling now loose. In fact everything splendid. Money became easy at once. Marks rose. Exports jumped. Gold reserve swelled.

3 p. m. Slightly bad news. Appears there is trouble in the Island of Piccolo Domingo. Looked it up on map. Is one of the smaller West Indies. We don't own it. I imagine Roosevelt must have overlooked it. An American has been in trouble there: was refused a drink after closing time and burnt down saloon. Is now in jail. Shall send at once our latest battleship—the *Woodrow*—new design, both ends alike, escorted by double-ended coal barges the *Wilson*, the *President*, the *Professor* and the *Thinker*. Shall take firm stand on American rights. Piccolo Domingo must either surrender the American alive, or give him to us dead.

TUESDAY. A lovely day. Rose early. Put flowers in all the vases. Laid a wreath of early japonica beside my egg-cup on the breakfast table. Cabinet to morning prayers and breakfast. Prayed for better guidance.

9 a. m. Trouble, bad trouble. First of all Roosevelt has an interview in the morning papers in which he asks why I don't treat Germany as I treat Piccolo Domingo. Now, what a fool question! Can't he *see* why? Roosevelt never could see reason. Bryan also has an interview: wants to know why I don't treat Piccolo Domingo as I treat Germany? Doesn't he *know* why?

Result: strained feeling in Washington. Morning mail bad.

10 a. m. British Admiralty communication. To the pigeon-house at once. They offer to send piece of torpedo, fragment of ship and selected portions of dead American citizens.

Have come out of pigeon-house. Have cabled back: How do they know it is a torpedo, how do they know it is a fragment, how do they know he was an American who said he was dead?

My answer has helped. Feeling in Washington easier at once. General buoyancy. Loans and discounts doubled.

As I expected—a note from Germany. Chancellor very explicit. Says not only did they not torpedo the *Torpid*, but that on the day (whenever it was) that the steamer was torpedoed they had no submarines at sea, no torpedoes in their submarines, and nothing really explosive in their torpedoes. Offers, very kindly, to fill in the date of sworn statement as soon as we furnish accurate date of incident. Adds that his own theory is that the *Torpid* was sunk by somebody throwing rocks at it from the shore. Wish, somehow, that he had not added this argument.

More bad news: Further trouble in Mexico. Appears General Villa is not dead. He has again crossed the border, shot up a saloon and retreated to the mountains of Huahuapaxtapetl. Have issued instructions to have the place looked up on the map and send the whole army to it, but without in any way violating the neutrality of Mexico.

Late cables from England. Two more ships torpedoed. American passenger lost. Name of Roosevelt. Christian name not Theodore but William. Cabled expression of regret.

WEDNESDAY. Rose sad at heart. Did not work in garden. Tried to weed a little grass along the paths but simply couldn't. This is a cruel job. How was it that Roosevelt grew stout on it? His nature must be different from mine. What a miserable nature he must have.

Received delegations. From Kansas, on the prospect of the corn crop: they said the number of hogs in Kansas will double. Congratulated them. From Idaho, on the blight on the root crop: they say there will soon not be a hog left in Idaho. Expressed my sorrow. From Michigan, beet sugar growers urging a higher percentage of sugar in beets. Took firm stand: said I stand where I stood and I stood where I stand. They went away dazzled, delighted.

Mail and telegrams. British Admiralty. *Torpid* Incident. Send further samples. Fragment of valise, parts of cow-hide trunk (dead passenger's luggage) which, they say, could not have been made except in Nevada.

Cabled that the incident is closed and that I stand where I stood and that I am what I am. Situation in Washington relieved at once. General feeling that I shall not make war.

Second Cable from England. The Two New Cases. Claim both ships torpedoed. Offer proofs. Situation very grave. Feeling in Washington very tense. Roosevelt out with a signed statement, *What will the President Do?* Surely he knows what I will do.

Cables from Germany. Chancellor now positive as to *Torpid*. Sworn evidence that she was sunk by some one throwing a rock. Sample of rock to follow. Communication also from Germany regarding the New Cases. Draws attention to fact that all of the crews who were not drowned were saved. An important point. Assures this government that everything ascertainable will be ascertained, but that pending juridical verification any imperial exemplification must be held categorically allegorical. How well these Germans write!

THURSDAY. A dull morning. Up early and read Congressional Government. Breakfast. Prayers. We prayed for the United States, for the citizens, for the Congress (both houses, especially the Senate), and for the Cabinet. Is there any one else?

Trouble. Accident to naval flotilla *en route* to Piccolo Domingo. The new battleship the *Woodrow* has broken down. Fault in structure. Tried to go with both ends first. Appeared impossible. Went sideways a little and is sinking. Wireless from the barges the *Wilson*, the *Thinker* and others. They are standing by. They wire that they will continue to stand by. Why on earth do they do that? Shall cable them to act.

Feeling in Washington gloomy.

FRIDAY. Rose early and tried to sweep out the White House. Had little heart for it. The dust gathers in the corners. How did Roosevelt manage to keep it so clean? An idea! I must get a vacuum cleaner! But where can I get a vacuum? Took my head in my hands and thought: problem solved. Can get the vacuum all right.

Good news. Villa dead again. Feeling in Washington relieved.

Trouble. Ship torpedoed. News just came from the French Government. Full-rigged ship, the *Ping-Yan*, sailing out of Ping Pong, French Cochin China, and cleared for Hoo-Ra, Indo-Arabia. No American citizens on board, but one American citizen with ticket left behind on wharf at Ping Pong. Claims damages. Complicated case. Feeling in Washington much disturbed. Sterling exchange fell and wouldn't get up. French Admiralty urge treaty of 1778. German Chancellor admits torpedoing ship but denies that it was full-rigged. Captain of submarine drew picture of ship as it sank. His picture unlike any known ship of French navy.

SATURDAY. A day of trouble. Villa came to life and crossed the border. Our army looking for him in Mexico: inquiry by wire, are they authorised to come back? General Carranza asks leave to invade Canada. Piccolo Domingo expedition has failed. The *Woodrow* is still sinking. The President and the *Thinker* cable that they are still standing by and will continue to stand where they have stood. British Admiralty sending shipload of fragments. German Admiralty sending shipload of affidavits. Feeling in Washington depressed to the lowest depths. Sterling sinking. Marks falling. Exports dwindling.

Further Foolishness

An idea: Is this job worth while? I wonder if Billy Sunday would take it?

Spent the evening watering the crocuses. Whoever is here a year from now is welcome to them. They tell me that Hughes hates crocuses. Watered them very carefully.

SUNDAY. Good news! Just heard from Princeton University. I am to come back, and everything will be forgiven and forgotten.

Timid Thoughts on Timely Topics

XVI. Are the Rich Happy?

Let me admit at the outset that I write this essay without adequate material. I have never known, I have never seen, any rich people. Very often I have thought that I had found them. But it turned out that it was not so. They were not rich at all. They were quite poor. They were hard up. They were pushed for money. They didn't know where to turn for ten thousand dollars.

In all the cases that I have examined this same error has crept in. I had often imagined, from the fact of people keeping fifteen servants, that they were rich. I had supposed that because a woman rode down town in a limousine to buy a fifty-dollar hat, she must be well to do. Not at all. All these people turn out on examination to be not rich. They are cramped. They say it themselves. Pinched, I think, is the word they use. When I see a glittering group of eight people in a stage box at the opera, I know that they are all pinched. The fact that they ride home in a limousine has nothing to do with it.

A friend of mine who has ten thousand dollars a year told me the other day with a sigh that he found it quite impossible to keep up with the rich. On his income he couldn't do it. A family that I know who have twenty thousand a year have told me the same thing. They can't keep up with the rich. There is no use trying. A man that I respect very much who has an income of fifty thousand dollars a year from his law practice has told me with the greatest frankness that he finds it absolutely impossible to keep up with the rich. He says it is better to face the brutal fact of being poor. He says he can only give me a plain meal, what he calls a home dinner —it takes three men and two women to serve it—and he begs me to put up with it.

As far as I remember, I have never met Mr. Carnegie. But I know that if I did he would tell me that he found it quite impossible to keep up with Mr. Rockefeller. No doubt Mr. Rockefeller has the same feeling.

On the other hand there are, and there must be rich people, somewhere. I run across traces of them all the time. The janitor in the building where I work has told me that he has a rich cousin in England who is in the South-Western Railway and gets ten pounds a week. He says the railway wouldn't know what to do without him. In the same way the lady who washes at my house has a rich uncle. He lives in Winnipeg and owns his own house, clear, and has two girls at the high school.

But these are only reported cases of richness. I cannot vouch for them myself.

When I speak therefore of rich people and discuss whether they are happy, it is understood that I am merely drawing my conclusions from the people whom I see and know.

My judgment is that the rich undergo cruel trials and bitter tragedies of which the poor know nothing.

In the first place I find that the rich suffer perpetually from money troubles. The poor sit snugly at home while sterling exchange falls ten points in a day. Do they care? Not a bit. An adverse balance of trade washes over the nation like a flood. Who have to mop it up? The rich. Call money rushes up to a hundred per cent, and the poor can still sit and laugh at a ten cent moving picture show and forget it.

But the rich are troubled by money all the time.

I know a man, for example—his name is Spugg—whose private bank account was overdrawn last month twenty thousand dollars. He told me so at dinner at his club, with apologies for feeling out of sorts. He said it was bothering him. He said he thought it rather unfair of his bank to have called his attention to it. I could sympathise, in a sort of way, with his feelings. My own account was overdrawn twenty cents at the time. I knew that if the bank began calling in overdrafts it might be my turn next. Spugg said he supposed he'd have to telephone his secretary in the morning to sell some bonds and cover it. It seemed an awful thing to have to do. Poor people are never driven to this sort of thing. I have known cases of their having to sell a little furniture, perhaps, but imagine having to sell the very bonds out of one's desk. There's a bitterness about it that the poor man can never know.

With this same man, Mr. Spugg, I have often talked of the problem of wealth. He is a self-made man and he has told me again and again that the wealth he has accumulated is a mere burden to him. He says that he was much happier when he had only the plain, simple things of life. Often as I sit at dinner with him over a meal of nine courses, he tells me how much he would prefer a plain bit of boiled pork with a little mashed turnip. He says that if he had his way he would make his dinner out of a couple of sausages, fried with a bit of bread. I forgot what it is that stands in his way. I have seen Spugg put aside his glass of champagne—or his glass after he had drunk his champagne—with an expression of something like contempt. He says that he remembers a running creek at the back of his father's farm where he used to lie at full length upon the grass and drink his fill. Champagne, he says, never tasted like that. I have suggested that he should lie on his stomach on the floor of the club and drink a saucerful of soda water. But he won't.

I know well that my friend Spugg would be glad to be rid of his wealth altogether, if such a thing were possible. Till I understood about these things, I always imagined that wealth could be given away. It appears that it cannot. It is a burden that one must carry. Wealth, if one has enough of it, becomes a form of social service. One regards it as a means of doing good to the world, of helping to brighten the lives of others—in a word, a solemn trust. Spugg has often talked with me so long and so late on this topic—the duty of brightening the lives of others—that the waiter who held blue flames for his cigarettes fell asleep against a door post, and the chauffeur outside froze to the seat of his motor.

Spugg's wealth, I say, he regards as a solemn trust. I have often asked him why he didn't give it, for example, to a college. But he tells me that unfortunately he is not a college man. I have called his attention to the need of further pensions for college professors; after all that Mr. Carnegie and others have done, there are still thousands and thousands of old professors of thirty-five and even forty, working away day after day and getting nothing but what they earn themselves, and with no provision beyond the age of eighty-five. But Mr. Spugg says that these men are the nation's heroes. Their work is its own reward.

But, after all, Mr. Spugg's troubles—for he is a single man with no ties—are in a sense selfish. It is perhaps in the homes, or more properly in the residences, of the rich that the great silent tragedies are being enacted every day—tragedies of which the fortunate poor know and can know nothing.

I saw such a case only a few nights ago at the house of the Ashcroft-Fowlers, where I was dining. As we went in to dinner, Mrs. Ashcroft-Fowler said in a quiet aside to her husband, "Has Meadows spoken? " He shook his head rather gloomily and answered, "No, he has said nothing yet. " I saw them exchange a glance of quiet sympathy and mutual help, like people in trouble, who love one another.

They were old friends and my heart beat for them. All through the dinner as Meadows—he was their butler—poured out the wine with each course, I could feel that some great trouble was impending over my friends.

After Mrs. Ashcroft-Fowler had risen and left us, and we were alone over our port wine, I drew my chair near to Fowler's and I said, "My dear Fowler, I'm an old friend and you'll excuse me if I seem to be taking a liberty. But I can see that you and your wife are in trouble. "

"Yes, " he said very sadly and quietly, "we are. "

"Excuse me, " I said. "Tell me—for it makes a thing easier if one talks about it—is it anything about Meadows? "

"Yes, " he said, "it is about Meadows. "

There was silence for a moment, but I knew already what Fowler was going to say. I could feel it coming.

"Meadows, " he said presently, constraining himself to speak with as little emotion as possible, "is leaving us. "

"Poor old chap! " I said, taking his hand.

"It's hard, isn't it? " he said. "Franklin left last winter—no fault of ours; we did everything we could —and now Meadows. "

There was almost a sob in his voice.

"He hasn't spoken definitely as yet, " Fowler went on, "but we know there's hardly any chance of his staying. "

"Does he give any reason? " I asked.

"Nothing specific, " said Fowler. "It's just a sheer case of incompatibility. Meadows doesn't like us. "

He put his hand over his face and was silent.

I left very quietly a little later, without going up to the drawing-room. A few days afterwards I heard that Meadows had gone. The Ashcroft-Fowlers, I am told, are giving up in despair. They are going to take a little suite of ten rooms and four baths in the Grand Palaver Hotel, and rough it there for the winter.

Yet one must not draw a picture of the rich in colours altogether gloomy. There are cases among them of genuine, light-hearted happiness.

I have observed this is especially the case among those of the rich who have the good fortune to get ruined, absolutely and completely ruined. They may do this on the Stock Exchange or by banking or in a dozen other ways. The business side of getting ruined is not difficult.

Once the rich are ruined, they are, as far as my observation goes, all right. They can then have anything they want.

I saw this point illustrated again just recently. I was walking with a friend of mine and a motor passed bearing a neatly dressed young man, chatting gaily with a pretty woman. My friend raised his hat and gave it a jaunty and cheery swing in the air as if to wave goodwill and happiness.

"Poor old Edward Overjoy! " he said, as the motor moved out of sight.

"What's wrong with him? " I asked.

"Hadn't you heard? " said my friend. "He's ruined—absolutely cleaned out—not a cent left. "

"Dear me! " I said. "That's awfully hard. I suppose he'll have to sell that beautiful motor? "

My friend shook his head.

"Oh, no, " he said. "He'll hardly do that. I don't think his wife would care to sell that. "

My friend was right. The Overjoys have not sold their motor. Neither have they sold their magnificent sandstone residence. They are too much attached to it, I believe, to sell it. Some people thought they would have given up their box at the opera. But it appears not. They are too musical to care to do that. Meantime it is a matter of general notoriety that the Overjoys are absolutely ruined; in fact, they haven't a single cent. You could buy Overjoy—so I am informed—for ten dollars.

But I observe that he still wears a seal-lined coat worth at least five hundred.

XVII. Humour as I See It

It is only fair that at the back of this book I should be allowed a few pages to myself to put down some things that I really think.

Until two weeks ago I might have taken my pen in hand to write about humour with the confident air of an acknowledged professional.

But that time is past. Such claim as I had has been taken from me. In fact I stand unmasked. An English reviewer writing in a literary journal, the very name of which is enough to put contradiction to sleep, has said of my writing, "What is there, after all, in Professor Leacock's humour but a rather ingenious mixture of hyperbole and myosis? "

The man was right. How he stumbled upon this trade secret I do not know. But I am willing to admit, since the truth is out, that it has long been my custom in preparing an article of a humorous nature to go down to the cellar and mix up half a gallon of myosis with a pint of hyperbole. If I want to give the article a decidedly literary character, I find it well to put in about half a pint of paresis. The whole thing is amazingly simple.

But I only mention this by way of introduction and to dispel any idea that I am conceited enough to write about humour, with the professional authority of Ella Wheeler Wilcox writing about love, or Eva Tanguay talking about dancing.

All that I dare claim is that I have as much sense of humour as other people. And, oddly enough, I notice that everybody else makes this same claim. Any man will admit, if need be, that his sight is not good, or that he cannot swim, or shoots badly with a rifle, but to touch upon his sense of humour is to give him a mortal affront.

"No, " said a friend of mine the other day, "I never go to Grand Opera, " and then he added with an air of pride, "You see, I have absolutely no ear for music. "

"You don't say so! " I exclaimed.

"None! " he went on. "I can't tell one tune from another. I don't know *Home, Sweet Home* from *God Save the King*. I can't tell whether a man is tuning a violin or playing a sonata. "

He seemed to get prouder and prouder over each item of his own deficiency. He ended by saying that he had a dog at his house that had a far better ear for music than he had. As soon as his wife or any visitor started to play the piano the dog always began to howl—plaintively, he said—as if it were hurt. He himself never did this.

When he had finished I made what I thought a harmless comment.

"I suppose, " I said, "that you find your sense of humour deficient in the same way: the two generally go together. "

My friend was livid with rage in a moment.

"Sense of humour! " he said. "My sense of humour! Me without a sense of humour! Why, I suppose I've a keener sense of humour than any man, or any two men, in this city! "

From that he turned to bitter personal attack. He said that *my* sense of humour seemed to have withered altogether.

He left me, still quivering with indignation.

Personally, however, I do not mind making the admission, however damaging it may be, that there are certain forms of so-called humour, or, at least, fun, which I am quite unable to appreciate. Chief among these is that ancient thing called the Practical Joke.

"You never knew McGann, did you? " a friend of mine asked me the other day.

When I said I had never known McGann, he shook his head with a sigh, and said:

"Ah, you should have known McGann. He had the greatest sense of humour of any man I ever knew—always full of jokes. I remember one night at the boarding-house where we were, he stretched a string across the passage-way and then rang the dinner bell. One of the boarders broke his leg. We nearly died laughing. "

"Dear me! " I said. "What a humorist! Did he often do things like that? "

"Oh, yes, he was at them all the time. He used to put tar in the tomato soup, and beeswax and tin-tacks on the chairs. He was full of ideas. They seemed to come to him without any trouble. "

McGann, I understand, is dead. I am not sorry for it. Indeed, I think that for most of us the time has gone by when we can see the fun of putting tacks on chairs, or thistles in beds, or live snakes in people's boots.

To me it has always seemed that the very essence of good humour is that it must be without harm and without malice. I admit that there is in all of us a certain vein of the old original demoniacal humour or joy in the misfortune of another which sticks to us like our original sin. It ought not to be funny to see a man, especially a fat and pompous man, slip suddenly on a banana skin. But it is. When a skater on a pond who is describing graceful circles, and showing off before the crowd, breaks through the ice and gets a ducking, everybody shouts with joy. To the original savage, the cream of the joke in such cases was found if the man who slipped broke his neck, or the man who went through the ice never came up again. I can imagine a group of prehistoric men standing round the ice-hole where he had disappeared and laughing till their sides split. If there had been such a thing as a prehistoric newspaper, the affair would have headed up: *"Amusing Incident. Unknown Gentleman Breaks Through Ice and Is Drowned. "*

But our sense of humour under civilisation has been weakened. Much of the fun of this sort of thing has been lost on us.

Children, however, still retain a large share of this primitive sense of enjoyment.

I remember once watching two little boys making snow-balls at the side of the street and getting ready a little store of them to use. As they worked, there came along an old man wearing a silk hat, and belonging by appearance to the class of "jolly old gentlemen. " When he saw the boys his gold spectacles gleamed with kindly enjoyment. He began waving his arms and calling, "Now, then, boys, free shot at me! free shot! " In his gaiety he had, without noticing it, edged himself over the sidewalk on to the street. An express cart collided with him and knocked him over on his back in a heap of snow. He lay there gasping and trying to get the snow off his face and spectacles. The boys gathered up their snow-balls and took a run toward him. "Free shot! " they yelled. "Soak him! Soak him! "

I repeat, however, that for me, as I suppose for most of us, it is a prime condition of humour that it must be without harm or malice, nor should it convey incidentally any real picture of sorrow or suffering or death. There is a great deal in the humour of Scotland (I admit its general merit) which seems to me not being a Scotchman, to sin in this respect. Take this familiar story (I quote it as something already known and not for the sake of telling it).

A Scotchman had a sister-in-law—his wife's sister—with whom he could never agree. He always objected to going anywhere with her, and in spite of his wife's entreaties always refused to do so. The wife was taken mortally ill and as she lay dying, she whispered, "John, ye'll drive Janet with you to the funeral, will ye no? " The Scotchman, after an internal struggle, answered, "Margaret, I'll do it for ye, but it'll spoil my day. "

Whatever humour there may be in this is lost for me by the actual and vivid picture that it conjures up—the dying wife, the darkened room and the last whispered request.

No doubt the Scotch see things differently. That wonderful people—whom personally I cannot too much admire—always seem to me to prefer adversity to sunshine, to welcome the prospect of a pretty general damnation, and to live with grim cheerfulness within the very shadow of death. Alone among the nations they have converted the devil —under such names as Old Horny—into a familiar acquaintance not without a certain grim charm of his own. No doubt also there enters into their humour something of the original barbaric attitude towards things. For a primitive people who saw death often and at first hand, and for whom the future world was a vivid reality that could be *felt*, as it were, in the midnight forest and heard in the roaring storm, it was no doubt natural to turn the flank of terror by forcing a merry and jovial acquaintance with the unseen world. Such a practice as a wake, and the merry-making about the corpse, carry us back to the twilight of the world, with the poor savage in his bewildered misery, pretending that his dead still lived. Our funeral with its black trappings and its elaborate ceremonies is the lineal descendant of a merry-making. Our undertaker is, by evolution, a genial master of ceremonies, keeping things lively at the death-dance. Thus have the ceremonies and the trappings of death been transformed in the course of ages till the forced gaiety is gone, and the black hearse and the gloomy mutes betoken the cold dignity of our despair.

But I fear this article is getting serious. I must apologise.

I was about to say, when I wandered from the point, that there is another form of humour which I am also quite unable to appreciate. This is that particular form of story which may be called, *par excellence*, the English Anecdote. It always deals with persons of rank and birth, and, except for the exalted nature of the subject itself, is, as far as I can see, absolutely pointless.

This is the kind of thing that I mean.

"His Grace the Fourth Duke of Marlborough was noted for the open-handed hospitality which reigned at Blenheim, the family seat, during his regime. One day on going in to luncheon it was discovered that there were thirty guests present, whereas the table only held covers for twenty-one. 'Oh, well, ' said the Duke, not a whit abashed, 'some of us will have to eat standing up. ' Everybody, of course, roared with laughter. "

My only wonder is that they didn't kill themselves with it. A mere roar doesn't seem enough to do justice to such a story as this.

The Duke of Wellington has been made the storm-centre of three generations of wit of this sort. In fact the typical Duke of Wellington story has been reduced to a thin skeleton such as this:

"A young subaltern once met the Duke of Wellington coming out of Westminster Abbey. 'Good morning, your Grace, ' he said, 'rather a wet morning. ' 'Yes' said the Duke, with a very rigid bow, 'but it was a damn sight wetter, sir, on the morning of Waterloo. ' The young subaltern, rightly rebuked, hung his head. "

Nor is it only the English who sin in regard to anecdotes.

One can indeed make the sweeping assertion that the telling of stories as a mode of amusing others ought to be kept within strict limits. Few people realise how extremely difficult it is to tell a story so as to reproduce the real fun of it—to "get it over" as the actors say. The mere "facts" of a story seldom make it funny. It needs the right words, with every word in its proper place. Here and there, perhaps once in a hundred times, a story turns up which needs no telling. The humour of it turns so completely on a sudden twist or incongruity in the *denouement* of it that no narrator, however clumsy, can altogether fumble it.

Take, for example, this well-known instance—a story which, in one form or other, everybody has heard.

"George Grossmith, the famous comedian, was once badly run down and went to consult a doctor. It happened that the doctor, though, like everybody else, he had often seen Grossmith on the stage, had never seen him without his make-up and did not know him by sight. He examined his patient, looked at his tongue, felt his pulse and tapped his lungs. Then he shook his head. 'There's nothing wrong with you, sir, ' he said, 'except that you're run down from overwork and worry. You need rest and amusement. Take a night off and go and see George Grossmith at the Savoy. ' 'Thank you, ' said the patient, 'I *am* George Grossmith. '"

Let the reader please observe that I have purposely told this story all wrongly, just as wrongly as could be, and yet there is something left of it. Will the reader kindly look back to the beginning of it and see for himself just how it ought to be narrated and what obvious error has been made? If he has any particle of the artist in his make-up, he will see at once that the story ought to begin:

"One day a very haggard and nervous-looking patient called at the house of a fashionable doctor, etc. etc. "

In other words, the chief point of the joke lies in keeping it concealed till the moment when the patient says, "Thank you, I am George Grossmith. " But the story is such a good one that it cannot be completely spoiled even when told wrongly. This particular anecdote has been variously told of George Grossmith, Coquelin, Joe Jefferson, John Hare, Cyril Maude, and about sixty others. And I have noticed that there is a certain type of man who, on hearing this story about Grossmith, immediately tells it all back again, putting in the name of somebody else, and goes into new fits of laughter over it, as if the change of name made it brand new.

But few people, I repeat, realise the difficulty of reproducing a humorous or comic effect in its original spirit.

"I saw Harry Lauder last night, " said Griggs, a Stock Exchange friend of mine, as we walked up town together the other day. "He came on to the stage in kilts" (here Grigg started to chuckle) "and he had a slate under his arm" (here Griggs began to laugh quite heartily), "and he said, 'I always like to carry a slate with me' (of course he said it in Scotch but I can't do the Scotch the way he does it) 'just in case there might be any figures I'd be wanting to put down'" (by this time, Griggs was almost suffocated with laughter)— "and he took a little bit-of chalk out of his pocket, and he said" (Griggs was now almost hysterical), "'I like to carry a wee bit chalk along because I find the slate is'" (Griggs was now faint with laughter) "'the slate is—is—not much good without the chalk. '"

Griggs had to stop, with his hand to his side, and lean against a lamp-post. "I can't, of course, do the Scotch the way Harry Lauder does it, " he repeated.

Exactly. He couldn't do the Scotch and he couldn't do the rich mellow voice of Mr. Lauder and the face beaming with merriment, and the spectacles glittering with amusement, and he couldn't do the slate, nor the "wee bit chalk"—in fact he couldn't do any of it. He ought merely to have said, "Harry Lauder, " and leaned up against a post and laughed till he had got over it.

Yet in spite of everything, people insist on spoiling conversation by telling stories. I know nothing more dreadful at a dinner table than one of these amateur raconteurs—except perhaps, two of them. After about three stories have been told, there falls on the dinner table an uncomfortable silence, in which everybody is aware that everybody else is trying hard to think of another story, and is failing to find it. There is no peace in the gathering again till some man of firm and quiet mind turns to his neighbour and says, "But after all there is no doubt that whether we like it or not prohibition is coming. " Then everybody in his heart says, "Thank heaven! " and the whole tableful are happy and contented again, till one of the story-tellers "thinks of another, " and breaks loose.

Worst of all perhaps is the modest story-teller who is haunted by the idea that one has heard this story before. He attacks you after this fashion:

"I heard a very good story the other day on the steamer going to Bermuda"—then he pauses with a certain doubt in his face—"but perhaps you've heard this? "

"No, no, I've never been to Bermuda. Go ahead. "

"Well, this is a story that they tell about a man who went down to Bermuda one winter to get cured of rheumatism —but you've heard this? "

"No, no. "

"Well he had rheumatism pretty bad and he went to Bermuda to get cured of it. And so when he went into the hotel he said to the clerk at the desk—but, perhaps you know this. "

"No, no, go right ahead. "

"Well, he said to the clerk, 'I want a room that looks out over the sea' —but perhaps—"

Now the sensible thing to do is to stop the narrator right at this point. Say to him quietly and firmly, "Yes, I have heard that story. I always liked it ever since it came out in *Tit Bits* in 1878, and I read it every time I see it. Go on and tell it to me and I'll sit back with my eyes closed and enjoy it. "

No doubt the story-telling habit owes much to the fact that ordinary people, quite unconsciously, rate humour very low: I mean, they underestimate the difficulty of "making humour. " It would never occur to them that the thing is hard, meritorious and dignified. Because the result is gay and light, they think the process must be. Few people would realise that it is much harder to write one of Owen Seaman's "funny" poems in *Punch* than to write one of the Archbishop of Canterbury's sermons. Mark Twain's *Huckleberry Finn* is a greater work than Kant's *Critique of Pure Reason,* and Charles Dickens's creation of Mr. Pickwick did more for the elevation of the human race—I say it in all seriousness—than Cardinal Newman's *Lead, Kindly Light, Amid the Encircling Gloom.* Newman only cried out for light in the gloom of a sad world. Dickens gave it.

But the deep background that lies behind and beyond what we call humour is revealed only to the few who, by instinct or by effort,

153

have given thought to it. The world's humour, in its best and greatest sense, is perhaps the highest product of our civilisation. One thinks here not of the mere spasmodic effects of the comic artist or the blackface expert of the vaudeville show, but of the really great humour which, once or twice in a generation at best, illuminates and elevates our literature. It is no longer dependent upon the mere trick and quibble of words, or the odd and meaningless incongruities in things that strike us as "funny. " Its basis lies in the deeper contrasts offered by life itself: the strange incongruity between our aspiration and our achievement, the eager and fretful anxieties of to-day that fade into nothingness to-morrow, the burning pain and the sharp sorrow that are softened in the gentle retrospect of time, till as we look back upon the course that has been traversed we pass in view the panorama of our lives, as people in old age may recall, with mingled tears and smiles, the angry quarrels of their childhood. And here, in its larger aspect, humour is blended with pathos till the two are one, and represent, as they have in every age, the mingled heritage of tears and laughter that is our lot on earth.

END

CPSIA information can be obtained at www.ICGtesting.com
Printed in the USA
LVOW06s1024230815

451200LV00003B/526/P